AWAKE

WE'RE NOT SO DIVIDED

RODGER CARLYLE

This is a work of fiction. For the purpose of the story, quotations from historical figures are included, along with actual events, institutions, agencies, and public offices. The characters are all based on real people.

AWAKE: WE'RE NOT SO DIVIDED. Copyright © 2022 by Rodger Carlyle. All rights reserved.

Published in the United States by Verity Books, an imprint of Comsult, LLC.

All rights reserved. Except for brief passages except quoted in newspaper, magazine, radio, television or online reviews, no portion of this book may be reproduced, distributed, or transmitted in any form or by any means, electronic or mechanical including photocopying, recording, or information storage or retrieval systems without the prior written permission of the author and/or Comsult, LLC.

First published in 2022.

ISBN 978-1-7379497-6-3 (e-book)
ISBN 978-1-7379497-5-6 (paperback)

Cover design and formatting: Damonza

1

HOW I MET MELODY

The protest in the park across from the governor's mansion had been rowdy and noisy, just what the organizers hoped for. The signs protesting the recent Supreme Court decision on abortion was supposed to be the focus, but small groups advertising grievances on dozens of issues carried signs and chanted slogans. As a writer, I had watched from the sidelines looking for people, real people and taking notes. These groups were even better than airports for studying humans, looking for interesting examples, models that someday might be developed into fictional characters in a novel. I'd just started to outline a political thriller, one where competing factions were forced to work together when they realized the very doctrine that allowed disagreement was at risk.

I'd also hoped that at least a few of the politicians in attendance would reach into their exploration of the constitution and address what I believed was the elephant in the room. You know, kind of a realistic starting point for the planned book. But all I heard was platitudes.

I'd taken the time to ready the Dobbs decision and to then

haul out my trusty pocket copy of the Constitution. While the Supreme Court decision was being blasted for outlawing abortion, what I'd read was that the decision really dealt with a different issue. But after years of observing American politics, I'd accepted that while a large block of the country saw all politics as local, there was also a block that demanded the Federal Government solve every problem. The court argued that the legislative branches of government were the correct place to solve social ills and desires, that is if individuals could not solve them themselves. Their decision was that the court had no constitutional role in what a woman could or could not do with a pregnancy unless it was to adjudicate a law passed by some legislative body. Of course, the half-dozen politicians in attendance didn't see the decision that way. Each had taken their ten minutes to blast conservative senators for approving the justices who had just upended what the court viewed as an unconstitutional decision a half century ago. Still, a couple of the most vocal politicos might be good characters.

But my observations were irrelevant to what I had just witnessed. And that wasn't why I was there. As the rally broke up, I closed my notebook and decided that 4:30 on a Saturday was the perfect time to review my notes over a cold beer, preferably a local pilsner or lager as my aging stomach objected from time to time to my favorite IPA. I settled into a large corner booth at a pub across from the park, taking my favored chair with my back to the corner and three empty chairs across from me. Back against the wall just like Wild Bill Hickok except for his last poker game. Normally, as the only patron I would have chosen a seat at the bar, but the place was empty, and I needed some room to spread out notes on possible characters.

∿

Six women carried their signs back to the parking lot two blocks from the Capital building.

"Well, that went well," offered a greying woman dressed in jeans and a college sweatshirt as she tossed her sign into the back of her Volvo. "The faculty meeting on Wednesday was all about how we overturn this ridiculous decision. Thanks to all of you for your efforts." Four other women added their signs before the college professor slammed the hatch on her car.

"How do you think that went? She asked of a late twentyish woman just dropping her leather bag into the passenger seat of her Subaru. "I mean, you're a reporter, Melody, what are you going to write?"

Melody stepped away from her open driver's door, turning toward the voice. She recognized the professor, Dr. Becka, as one of her former mentors, one who had really helped shape her thinking. Brushing a loose strand of light tan hair from her face she couldn't help but smile. "That rally will be my top story tomorrow. You all did a great job of organizing. How you feel about this anti-woman decision came booming through. It helped to have folks from 'Black Lives Matter' and the 'Equity Justice Project' supporting you. The system needs a reboot."

"But did we move the needle? If the legislature attempts to push through anti-abortion legislation, can we build enough opposition to stop it until we can get Congress to pass national legislation?"

Melody absently-mindedly leaned against the fender of her yellow hatchback before catching herself. She'd forgotten how dirty her car was after her backcountry trip with two friends the day before. She slapped at what she knew was a layer of dust on her dark brown sweater and black jeans. "I don't know," she answered. "We had an editorial meeting last week. My editor is a strong progressive, but also a pragmatist. He asked us to start looking for some feedback from the other side. One of his favorite themes is that it isn't very interesting to write about people in an echo chamber. You can't move the needle if you are only talking to people who believe what you already believe."

The five women around the Volvo all stopped what they were doing and stared.

The professor shook her head. "There is no justification for greed and hate. If I wanted to listen to the opposition, I would turn on Fox News." She pressed a button on her key fob, locking her car. "I need a glass of wine. Anyone want to join me?"

"You're our ride home," replied the much younger head of a local non-profit that focused on homeless issues. "I'm in."

"Care to join us, Melody?" asked the professor. "I'm curious about how you can even consider writing about what people who just don't give a damn think. We need to find a way to either reeducate them or get them the hell out of the way."

By the time the women reached the pub, it was filling up fast.

✑

I watched as six women, including two who I knew were organizers of the rally marched through the door, looking for an empty table. The youngest one, the girl-next-door blond was one of the people who I'd studied at the rally. I wasn't quite sure what character she might represent some day, but unlike most of the people there, she had remained quiet and from time to time seemed to be narrating the event into her phone.

I noted that the only open table was the one next to me, so I waived and pointed toward it.

"Take the extra chairs," I offered as the women crowded around an identical table to mine. I slid my notes into more of a pile, while I concentrated on filling in my recollections of a zealous red-haired, middle-aged woman with a double-sided sign; one side screamed about the fascist court and the other with three huge letters, D E

I, which I knew referred to diversity, equity, and inclusion. From the moment she'd arrived she was a blur in the crowd, in the face of anyone who would tolerate her. My planned story might need one additional character.

For the next two hours, two beers and one order of loaded tater tots, I used my imagination to fill in what I didn't know about the six people that I'd signaled out of the crowd. I liked to actually discuss my notes with those I used as character models but found that most of my subjects only wanted to talk about their feelings, not themselves.

Now, I'm a retired businessman and politically non-affiliated, a man whose politics would generally be described as somewhat libertarian. I am also a student of history and a political scientist by education. I like to write about snippets of history that just don't add up, usually some incident where what the powerful wanted went all to hell and was then covered up. I am no fan of the elites, but even less of a fan of government bungling. But as much as I tried to focus on my character studies, the tone of the women next to me and their anger at just about everything in society and their deep-seated belief that government, especially the courts could right all wrongs surprised me.

The women all drank white wine, except for the blond woman who'd ordered a beer to go with a chef's salad, the only food on the table.

I had just about decided that I needed more quiet to complete my work when a cell phone rang. The woman in the university sweatshirt answered, held a short conversation, and then stood, announcing, "If you need a ride, you need to drink up. I need to get home."

Like shorebirds, five of the women rose as one. They picked up separate checks from the table and headed for the cashier, leaving the blond woman staring, her fork of lettuce dangling.

"Let me know if I can get you any more materials for your story, Melody," offered the professor as she dug out her credit card.

I waited a few minutes, thinking this might be an opportunity to flesh in some detail on one of my character models by actually talking to one.

"So, you are a writer?" I asked when the woman finally looked over at me. "I'm a fiction writer, but one who loves to use history and current events as the basis for what I write. I overheard someone say you are a writer as well."

"I'm a feature reporter for both the paper and a regional magazine." She answered. She took a minute to study the papers on my table. "What are you working on?"

I explained how I did character research, recalling how one woman at an airport, a woman so full of anguish that nobody would go near her had turned into a critical character in one of my books. "I'd like to learn more personal detail about those I think might be great characters, make them more real, but I seldom get the opportunity. When I ask, most are uncomfortable around someone who might have different opinions. We've retreated into silos of like-minded people."

"I get it," replied the woman. "My name is Melody and one of my assignments is to dig out why so many people refuse to accept that the system is rigged against most of us, especially minority groups and the poor. When I approach a lot of businesspeople and self-proclaimed conservative leaders, they just shake their head and turn away. Either that or they go on the attack."

With six decades of life behind me, many in business before I turned to writing, I recognized an opportunity when I saw one.

"Would you like to join me? Maybe we can help each other."

Melody emptied her beer, then picked up her salad plate and slid it onto my table. She swiveled her high bar stool to face me and smiled. "We can try," she said, "but you need to know that I have pretty strong feelings about what is happening in America today, and I love a good debate." She held her empty beer glass up and signaled the waitress that she wanted another.

I used the time it took for her new beverage to arrive to digest what I'd just heard. "You know, Melody, may I call you Melody?" She nodded as she chewed a bite of salad. "You know you might have just hit on why we are both struggling."

She nodded, encouraging me to go on, a great tool to keep people talking when they are offering something that might be important, a lawyer's tool and a good writer's tactic.

"Maybe, we both tend to open conversations in a way to encourage debate. I know that I can be more than a little pushy about my beliefs. I'm reminded of a Robert Frost quotation, 'People have to think, that's not to agree or disagree, that's voting."

"I don't know your name," she replied.

"Rodger with more than one last name depending on whether it serves me to use my pen name or not."

"Well, Rodger, perhaps we should try to have a discussion then, not a debate, just an exchange of ideas."

I sorted through my notes and found my minimal observations on Melody. Sliding them across the table I opened with, "Perhaps we can start with you helping me fill in some blanks on yourself."

Melody's face turned a bit blank, obviously uncomfortable.

"Or" I offered, "you can give me a list of subjects that might help your story. If I'm not the right one to comment, I'll bet I know someone who can."

She relaxed. "Okay, but no talking heads or academic experts. If I wanted their opinions, I'd buy their book."

"I'm more than a little partial to what common men believe myself," I answered. "No matter how bad things get, in the real world, superman is not coming to the rescue. Most common men and women, when faced with crises, probably have a cape of their own in their closet."

Melody put down her fork and sipped a bit of her Blue Moon with a slice of orange, looking over the top of her glass at me. "Why are so many people so fond of capitalism when socialism is more equitable? Why is wealth so important and for that matter, what is real wealth? Isn't economic justice a greater responsibility? I mean, racial and economic equality never seem to get better. For that matter, how does anyone help the economy as a whole? How does one improve their personal or family financial situation? Great family wealth seems really bad for the economy. The fat cats ignore those in need."

My response took some time and about half of my remaining beer.

"Don't you have any pre-scripted answers?" Melody asked.

"Well, ma'am, you just challenged me to recite from memory the entire history of America's economy, and probably the world's." I paused, and added, "I see why many might give you a thousand-yard stare after that opening."

"It just isn't fair that black family wealth is only a fraction of that of white families. Rich people pass on their wealth. That gives their kids a huge leg up over poor people. Inherited wealth is just plain wrong."

Melody was not the quiet observer that I'd watched, and she was just winding up. "Which opens a new area we need to discuss. Why are so many of you so determined to follow a constitution written by a bunch of old white slave owners two hundred years ago? It needs to be updated to meet today's societal changes. And the courts need to offer remedies for the racist laws based on that outdated document, they need to reinterpret it to fit today."

"Oh." There was no stopping this now.

She continued. "So many call America an exceptional country, but it is filled with inequality and huge gaps in social justice. We aren't far removed from the mindset of slaves and slave owners and workers as pawns who only create wealth for those already rich. And our system hasn't changed for 200 years. The rich people of this country only rebelled from England because the British were about to outlaw slavery."

By now I was furiously taking notes. My inclination was to cut my losses and get the hell out of there, but I'd been the one to open a dialog, and accepted her idea of a conversation. Mahatma Gandhi once said, "Honest disagreement is often a good sign of progress," I replied. I paused, but she was through.

"Anything else we need to cover besides human history for the last 4,000 years?" I knew that was a little confrontational, but I was struggling to keep it to a little confrontational. I needn't have worried; Melody had run her course and didn't even hear me. I waited for her to look up.

"I was right, I am not the one to answer all of your questions. I can handle some of what you are looking for, that is if you really want answers, if I wouldn't be wasting your time. And it is going to take some time since to really address your concerns I am going to have to introduce you to three or four others with better answers than I have."

She looked at me and smiled. "My stories will run for the next six weeks, so I have the time."

"Great, let's get started on Tuesday, there is someone I want you to meet, someone who is a great hands-on expert on the economy. I'll set it up. Now, your turn. Tell me about yourself young lady."

"You know that term young lady is condescending. Next you will want to pay for my salad and hold the door for me when I leave."

"Guilty. When I grew up, those were all things a gentleman did, they were part of what my single mom called manners. But I'll try to control it while we work together. Now, tell me about Melody, your background, your education and what you like to do. Beyond your strong feelings, what makes you tick."

"Tuesday works for me." She handed me her card. "Just call me and tell me where and when to meet you. I'll bring you a short resume when we meet."

I handed Melody my card which included a reference to my writing website. "I'll call my buddy tomorrow morning and see if we can get with him on Tuesday. I'll call you. Remember, I'm only going to ask him to discuss the economy. I've some other people in mind for the rest of your list, but it may take a while to set it all up."

2
MELODY MEETS BARRY

I forwarded Melody's list of topics to an old friend, Barry Salazar. He and I first connected while I was starting my first communications company and Barry and his sister were catering our monthly Friday get togethers. That had been about thirty years ago. I'd taken time to make my own notes on the one-page memo Melody sent me. We only had two hours of Barry's time, so keeping the conversation moving was critical.

We found him in his office above his flagship restaurant, SALAZARS SOUTH AMERICAN. His office was in the corner of a new two-story glass and tile building that covered a quarter of a city block. Across town was a second restaurant that catered to American and Tex-Mex tastes and across four states were more than three dozen fast food places. Each was fronted by a sign with a compass in the center and the letters NASA, which was an abbreviation from the old catering company, North American South American catering; a logo that was hard to forget.

Barry was a no-nonsense guy, and I was a bit surprised by his quiet and gracious reception. "It's good to finally meet you," he offered to Melody. "I've been impressed by a number of your stories over the last couple of years."

Melody smiled, and thanked him, but she was all business. "If we can, I'd like to use our time to really explore your thoughts on the economy."

Barry, pointed at some chairs in the corner of his office. "I hate to talk to anyone across a desk." He joined us, pointing out coffee, water, and some Mexican pastries on a tray. "Where would you like to start?"

"Rodger says you are a huge champion of capitalism, and I can see that you personally are doing just fine," began Melody. "But you're rich. You have hundreds of employees. A lot of them don't make enough to pay rent in the cities where they live. How do you justify that?"

"Allow me to tell you my story," he answered. "My father was a Cuban refugee who fled Castro. My mother was from Guatemala. Her family fled a militaristic government. One parent was fleeing socialism and the other a right-wing junta. Both were fleeing dictatorships. My father who had been a college professor found work as a doorman in a big hotel. My mother was a nurse but spoke little English, so she took a job as a maid in the same hotel. When I came along, and then my sister and my brother, they both had moved up in the hotel, both into entry level management but each insisted on continuing working shifts, to stay in touch with their workers. They pooled their salaries and managed to rent a small three-bedroom apartment within walking distance of work. We lived in a building with a lot of people who would not have survived without public assistance, and in the first years after they had children, my folks needed a little help. But I remember my mother's irritation when a social worker would visit us and question how we lived, how my parents spent money, and their strict control over my siblings and me."

Barry sipped from a cup of coffee that without cream would curl your toes. "With that as background, let me try to answer your first question."

"Okay, how about we start with, why you believe in capitalism."

"The late Walter E. Williams, a renowned economist and professor of economics at George Mason University once commented, **Capitalism is relatively new in human history. Prior to Capitalism, the way people amassed great wealth was by looting and plundering and enslaving their fellow man. Capitalism made it possible to become wealthy by serving your fellow man.**" Barry leaned back in his chair and tugged his tie.

I'd never seen Barry wear a tie before.

"My father, a college professor, was from a family who had put together a large farm over four generations. My dad studied history and economics and he would have loved that quotation. He watched the socialist government of Cuba decide that his family farm of about four hundred acres was more than any family should own, so the government took it and divided it up amongst the workers, all but the best part, overlooking the ocean. That land went to three party officials and two generals who helped put Fidel into power. When my father objected, he was demoted from department head in his university and when he refused to shut up, was removed from his teaching. That's when he fled Cuba."

"I can see his anger over the government taking what he thought was his, but didn't it help the workers?"

"Within five years, the only part of the farm that produced anything beyond what it took for a family to live on was the part that my grandparents retained. The money crops that fed Havana weren't even being planted. About half of the land lay fallow because the equipment that used to till the soil sat rusting because there was no one to coordinate its use or maintenance. The former farm workers still had food on the table, but no cash income. The government's solution was to seize the rest of our land and then cut the property into even smaller plots which did nothing to feed people in the cities. My grandparents took the pittance they were paid for their land and moved to Mexico."

"So, you think that the lives of the workers didn't improve?"

"Not much, if at all, and as the impact of the nationalization took effect on Cuba's industry, the same thing happened, the people's lives stayed the same. Cubans are trapped in the 1960's. None of the gains made in most of the world are available in Cuba. For a lot of people things got really bad. That lesson was not lost on me or my siblings."

"So, how did you get rich?"

I knew Barry's company was worth millions, but he didn't consider himself rich.

Barry looked over at me and began to laugh. "My parents kept all the tips they made in the hotel and used the money to give each of their kids $10,000 for college when they graduated from high school. I found that it wasn't enough for school in Florida, but I could move to the Midwest and attend junior college for $2500 tuition per year. I had to eat and pay rent, so I borrowed five-hundred dollars from family and armed with my mother's recipes I opened a catering business. It paid the rent and when I moved on to get my bachelor's degree two years later, I turned the business over to my best employee and started a second catering business here. When I graduated, instead of using my business degree in some big company, I just focused on what was already working. I started climbing what I call the ladder."

"Your employees can't afford to live on what you pay them. How do you justify that?"

"I didn't start off rich. I started at the bottom, cooking, serving, washing dishes. As the business grew, I looked for help, for people willing to do what I did, start at the bottom. I realized that the only thing they, like me, had to sell was time. Oh, they worked with their hands, and legs, and their heads, and applied what they already had learned, but in the end the only thing they had to sell me was time. You cannot manufacture more time, there are only so many hours in the day. So, I looked for people who felt trapped into selling their time with no upward prospects and opened a new door for them." Barry looked over at me and laughed. "Rodger's story on entry level work is better than mine. You need to hear it."

I was a bit embarrassed, unprepared to be an active participant, but I owed Barry for making his time available. "When I was just a kid, I worked at picking strawberries. The job entailed bending over or kneeling between two rows of strawberries on a hot day and carefully combing through each plant for ripe berries, picking them, and putting them in small cups in what they called a flat. You got paid for delivering a full 'flat' of berries to a truck that would take them to a processor. I was maybe nine at the time and in good shape, but still within twenty minutes my legs cramped and my back ached. It gave me great respect for the people in the fields who made a living doing this work. That summer taught me that I didn't want to do this my whole life. My single mom was always strapped for cash, so if I wanted much more than food, clothing, and shelter, earning it was up to me.

My first delivery was almost my last as the foreman took one look at my work and offered, "The cups are only 2/3 full and half of the berries in those cups are still too green to process. Just leave that flat on the ground, pick up another and pick berries that we can sell." I could tell by the look on his face, that me continuing my career as a berry picker would probably only continue if my second flat passed muster. Today some people would call that second chance white privilege just because of my skin, but after every day picking berries my pant knees were worn, my hands were

scratched, and I was exhausted just like everyone else in the fields."
Barry picked up the conversation where I left off.

"In piece work, like picking berries and being paid only for what you produce, one of three things happens. You fail to get very good at the job and you starve or change jobs. Or you study how others are doing the job and become more efficient so that you can make some money. The third thing that might happen is that after you pick for a while, you develop some personal skills and techniques that allow you to do the job more efficiently and you make okay money for someone who only has time to sell. The employer cares, but it isn't critical to them, because they aren't paying for your time, just the production from you investing your time.

I looked for people in that kind of job and offered them an opportunity to move beyond selling manual labor. In my business we still have entry level people, but our company invests in training them, so we are vested in seeing them succeed. If they don't produce, that gives us nothing to sell. But most do, and the more we train them, the more they produce and the more they increase profitability, which allows us to pay them more. But if you do not grow, become better in the restaurant business, remain a 'me too' employee, your value is only as good as the person we can hire to replace you. To many, this work seems lowly and to someone who has an elevated sense of self-importance, demeaning. Nonsense, this is where most people start and get their initial training and skills. Most senior executives start at the bottom. Smart, rich business owners start their kids at the most menial jobs. They sweep floors or load trucks. My kids started bussing tables and washing dishes. It gave them a foundation and understanding of the business and an appreciation for even the entry level employees."

Melody had been recording most of the conversation. I watched as she put her phone down and began scribbling on her old-fashioned pad. "How does grooming your own children help your employees?"

"One of the best ways to improve your lot at the restaurant is to study what you and others are doing and then come up with a better way to do the job. Not only are you more valuable, but you might help everyone else be better. The business produces more, in the same amount of time, can handle more customers, and probably makes a little more money. One thing for sure, you will get noticed. While everyone may get a little more pay because improved efficiency means the employer can afford it, you may end up on the short list for any coming promotion or with a new position based on your idea. Any employer, even me, will exploit what you created, and it will probably make your life a bit better, or a lot better. You will experience the value of improved productivity, and you earn the increase. No one gave you anything. You put your head into your time. My employees see my kids doing the same work as them.

Remember, most employers are counting on their employees getting better. They know that the most productive employees earn them more. They also know that motivated employees come up with ideas that make the whole operation better." He paused, chin resting in his hand.

"But I didn't answer your question about my own kids. Any person running a successful business that hopes to pass the business on to their heirs needs to make sure they are ready. I want my kids to understand every part of the business. But even more, like in my early days, I want them to understand and respect the employees that make it all work. They need to understand each operation and the people, to be aware of those who make things work better and to open a career path for them. What they learn will stick with them even if they go elsewhere."

Barry offered each of us more coffee. He was on a roll but

wanted to make sure that he was answering Melody's questions. "Is this becoming clear?"

"I'm still not sure how all this helps employees who can't pay their rent?"

"Entry level work is just that, a place to begin, to learn. My employees came up with almost every improvement that allowed us to grow. Some outgrow our small company, and that's great, I love to see them move on and succeed. One came in without a high school diploma, worked to get his GED, and then enrolled in college. He got more done in an hour than many of his peers did in two. We helped him with tuition and less than a year after graduating in supply-chain management, he came back to us with a truly innovative way of restructuring our ordering and supply to the two restaurants. We used his plan to open the fast-food outlets you see around the country. He now runs that division as president of his own group. He went from minimum wage to a mid-six figure income in fifteen years." Barry pointed to a picture on the wall.

"Another employee learned from him. She is now a vice-president of a major hotel chain, responsible for supporting their restaurants. A third, left us. She never really liked Latin food but had a passion for eastern European cuisine. She now owns four restaurants in the Pacific Northwest. The key is to bust it from the beginning, put what you have into the hours we pay you for, and climb the business ladder. Start with a move to entry level management and go from there. Every one of our fast-food outlets is a franchise owned by the manager, and every one of them started with us somewhere else. All but a handful started at the bottom."

Barry paused and smiled at Melody. "Entry level means entry level, it isn't supposed to be a career. Work hard, work smart, move up the ladder. If you are worried about someone else charting your success, if you expect government or someone else to take care of you, you miss the most important lesson of our system, YOU OWN

YOU, and you have choices your entire life. YOU OWN YOU, and it's up to you to create your future." Barry looked at his watch. "We've only covered a little from your list, and I have to cut this off. I have a school play to attend. But if you'd like, I can reschedule and even arrange for you to talk to some of our employees."

"Before we break up, one final question. How is this all better than socialism?

"Under socialism, the production of all is shared by all. There is no incentive to be more productive or to innovate. If all the candle makers during the 1800s shared all their work, even if they increased production, we wouldn't have electric lights. If one candle maker produces 100 candles a day more than the average candle maker, his family's standard of living isn't improved. If he does it because he invents better production methods, he becomes a threat to those who aren't innovative. Under capitalism he is rewarded."

Barry paused before adding. "That ladder we talked about; everyone on it is part of a system. From entry level to supervisor to manager to executive, everybody is both helping and taking advantage of each other. Some go on to be presidents of huge companies. Some become very wealthy. Some get to a level where they have enough to support a life other than their career that is more important. Wealth is what you want it to be, and that's not always money."

As Melody and I walked toward our cars, I asked, "Did you get what you wanted from that discussion?"

"I still don't think it's fair," replied Melody. "Some people aren't as motivated; others do not have the skills. Large groups are not really prepared. What does society owe them?"

"You will learn that I love historical quotations. For example, Mark Twain's, '**Don't go around saying the world owes you a living. The world owes you nothing. It was here first.**'"

Melody reached into her small portfolio. "I promised you a

resume. Here. You said you have three other people I need to talk to. Call me when it is set up."

I started to open her car door for her but didn't. Then she was gone. I slid into the front seat of my Dodge pickup and opened the envelope I'd just received.

Name: Melody Johnson

Age: 27

Education: Benington State University, BA in Liberal Arts with an emphasis in philosophy

UC Berkley, MA, Journalism

Affiliations: Sierra Club, International Federation of Journalists

Activities: Anything outdoors, hiking and rock climbing, river sports, softball

I participate in community and statewide social and economic justice activities that don't compromise my journalistic credibility.

That was it. Not much there to develop a profile from, but I was going to spend several more hours with Melody and hoped to flesh in enough to use her as a model for a fictional protagonist. I didn't necessarily agree with her politics, but she passionately cared about people.

Two days later, only a couple of hours before I was planning to introduce Melody to another source, I picked up the morning paper. There under her byline was her first article, *LOCAL RESTAURANTEUR ARGUES HE DOESN'T EXPLOIT WORKERS.*

If I had stopped reading there, I probably wouldn't have continued with the planned meeting, but her article, despite the headline, reasonably recounted our meeting with Barry.

3

MELODY MEETS LISA

We started our next interview with a short meeting at Melody's favorite coffee shop. "I read your article," I started just as my phone rang. It was Barry, and it would have been impossible to cover up his hysterical laugh over my cell.

"Just wanted to catch up with you, old friend," he started as he suppressed his laugh. "The opening of that reporter's story could have been the opening of a conversation with my own daughter last year or a half dozen with employees over the last couple of years. If I had thin skin, I could believe that I was Satan himself. Still, her story was fairly factual. Please pass on my congratulations for a reasonable portrayal of how I run my business."

"I heard him," said Melody before I could relay his message.

"So, today we look at the next steps in Barry's ladder," I said. "Barry became an entrepreneur in his twenties and then went beyond that to what you probably would call a capitalist. We're going to talk to a woman this morning that really understands what that means. Do you know Lisa Renfro?"

"No, but I think she runs some kind of non-profit organization."

"She's the CEO of CENTAMERICA, a large regional foundation. Its sole reason for being is to receive funds from wealthy families and companies and put it to work for good." I pulled out my copy of our original notes. "You seem to believe that wealth itself is bad, and inherited wealth is really bad. Lisa is someone who really understands this stuff."

Melody picked up her coffee and stood up. "Before we go, just one thing about our meeting with Mr. Salazar. Does he really believe that it's reasonable for everyone to want to push their way up that ladder?"

"No, and Barry understands that those on cruise-control won't move up." I paused.

"Barry is successful because he deals with what is in front of him, but, if you don't mind another of my quotations, I'd like to give you my thoughts."

Melody gave my one of those, *if I have to listen, I will,* smile.

"George Bernard Shaw, the famous playwright and political activist once offered, **'The reasonable man adapts himself to the world; the unreasonable one persists in trying to adapt the world to himself. Therefore, all progress depends on the unreasonable man.'"**

I think we all have a little of that unreasonable man in us. Some just let it out, let it run. Barry is one of those people and, like most really successful businesspeople, he surrounds himself with people who are more knowledgeable and smarter than him." I picked up my plain decaf coffee and popped the lid on it. "Lisa's office is only a couple of blocks from here."

We met Lisa Renfro in a nice conference room just down the hall from the entry to her foundation's leased offices. I hadn't seen Lisa in a year since I had helped her with recruiting for her eight-person board. She'd been desperate to find one board member from the arts. She was already waiting for us as the receptionist ushered us into the room.

Lisa was in her early fifties, brunette, fit, and dressed in a blue business suit with a white silk blouse that probably cost about as much as one of my books earns in royalties each month. Her appearance was about what you'd expect to find on Madison Avenue in the executive suite of a Wall Street Banking firm, which is where she came from. She extended her hand to Melody and just looked at me and pointed at a chair. "Rodger, we need to discuss your trust, sometime."

Turning to Melody she began, "So you want to know about wealth," she started. "I've been around wealthy people for two decades and most of them are not a lot different than the population as a whole. Some are a joy to be around, generous, and caring. Some are complete asses. Most are a mixture of good and bad. What is always good is their money if it is directed to good purposes."

Melody seemed at a loss for words, and Lisa was enough of a pro to remain silent until the reporter sorted out her thoughts.

"Here is my main objection," said Melody. "Rich people pass on their wealth to their children who then have a huge advantage over people from working class families and especially minorities and the poor. How can that be justified?"

I knew that Lisa was the right person for this conversation when she responded with a question. "What is wealth?"

"You know, more money than you need. Big yachts and summer homes in Florida. Nice, but for most people not something that they ever expect to own. Most people are just trying to pay their bills. Why shouldn't the system get most of that money when someone dies to help others? Rich kids don't start at the bottom."

"Wealth means different things to different people. To many, it means possessions, but to more it means the resources that allow them to do what they want in life. Great wealth funds the arts, music and things that make life richer. Our foundation has more than 100 trusts to fund everything from scholarships to medical research, to theater. Most are funded by contributions from numerous people with similar interests. Some are funded by individuals or families. But one thing is the same in all of them, their wealth all comes from some kind of business. Can we diverge a moment to discuss business?"

Melody nodded her head as she added some written notes to the recording she was making.

"Being wealthy does not mean that you have piles of cash. What it normally means is that you own a business or real estate that has capital value. Let's assume a family manufacturing business, making the proverbial widget. Let's say they have 500 employees, and the owner dies. The only cash in that business is the money to pay for its operations with some put away to cover emergencies. All of that is what we call retained earnings, profits. What would you do with that business when the owner dies, give it to government? Government can't run itself efficiently so if that is the answer, you might just as well fire all of the employees right away since the firm will fail. Or should we encourage the inheritors to minimize any inheritance tax liability by converting some of the equity to debt by borrowing against the company value and putting it into trusts to help society, then pay their legal taxes, placing the rest into the bank to fund ongoing operations. Since the time of kings and queens, when we buried them with gold, wealth does not ever disappear. It just shifts from one person to others and keeps on providing jobs and value to the society. One way to ensure that a firm survives the loss of a founder is for that owner to issue stock so that when they go, only a portion of the value is held by them. Probably the rest is owned by heirs or employees, or the public. To avoid paying estate taxes, many owners entrust their stock to people like us who convert it to cash and use it to do really good things. Most importantly the business continues and since the only way a business succeeds is to produce goods or services that society is willing to pay for, that help people, that business and its employees continue to serve society."

"But we never hear of wealthy people really doing good things with their wealth," replied Melody.

"You mean you don't write about it. You should and there are numerous examples. How about a man whose wealth dwarfed all of his contemporaries? Andrew Carnegie was a businessman and industrialist in the heyday of America's industrial revolution. He was by far the richest man in the nation. His rough and aggressive business practices created a monopoly in steel when it was critical to building world infrastructure. He was feared and hated by many, especially competitors, and an enigma to the public.

Before his death, he committed to giving away all of what was at that time the greatest fortune in the world. He sold his company by offering stock to everyone. His wife was committed to help, and they did. They built and endowed thousands of museums and public libraries not only in the U.S., but across the English-speaking world. Carnegie funded trusts and endowments for the arts, universities, libraries, public giving, even world peace. Carnegie projects and trusts are still helping the world a century after his death. He gave it all away under his moto, 'The man who dies thus rich, dies disgraced.'

In today's world, he would have been able to accomplish a lot less because those who believe that they have better ideas on how to spend Carnegie's wealth, wealth that they believe he probably didn't really deserve, would have taxed much of it away. Half of what they took would be lost to the bureaucrats."

"You don't give the government much credit for doing good," offered Melody. The government has hundreds of programs to help the less fortunate and victims of societal abuse."

"Overhead, the cost of administrating any organization's efforts to accomplish something is more than twice as high in government run programs as in privately funded programs. In other words, if government taxes a billionaire a million dollars to support a federal food program, generally as much as one half of that is lost to administration and only $500,000 puts food on the table. If the billionaire gives the same million dollars to a food bank directly, more than $800,000 actually goes to food. If he puts the same amount into an education or training program to help people develop skills to advance themselves, the money creates positive results, people get good jobs, and the beneficiaries buy the food they want."

"But will the wealthy help? Don't we need government to tell them to help, demand it through taxation?" asked Melody.

"Before the 1940's, churches and local beneficial societies helped the less fortunate. Hospitals raised funds to provide healthcare to those in need. It didn't take 60,000 employees in the Federal Department of Health and Human Services and an additional 100,000 in the 50 State departments to serve the less fortunate. Those receiving aid in the old days were determined to find work and then contribute back to the same groups that gave them a hand up."

We were interrupted by a young man who burst through the door, juggling a tray with coffee and cups. "Sorry Lisa," he offered as he put the tray in front of us, "I got tied up interviewing a farmer who just walked into the office with a check for $25,000. He was setting up his retirement and wanted to put it to work for some good cause."

As I poured coffee for the three of us, Lisa pointed to a framed poster on the wall. It was a quotation from the renowned economist Milton Friedman and read, **"One of the mistakes is to judge policies and programs by their intent instead of their results."**

"That saying applies to what we do here," said Lisa, "and to government. But government is terrible at actually producing results because it lacks a feedback loop. What I mean is that in government there is nobody looking over their shoulder to make sure they spend the money wisely and get any real return for it. Instead, the bureaucracy, once started, just keeps on going with the primary goal of being funded again and again. Did you know that the agency created to try to get Americans to wear seatbelts in the 1950's still exists? It has evolved but must find a new problem every year, so the employees keep their jobs. They cannot exist without developing new problems."

Melody loaded her coffee up with cream and then looked over at me. "I like the part about the Carnegies," she said, but that's old news. Nice for background, but hardly relevant in our modern society."

"I personally like the story of a contemporary wealthy family," I answered. "Leon Cooperman and his wife Toby live in Florida in a multi-million-dollar home, much of the cost covered by appreciation from selling a modest home they'd lived in for decades. They drive old cars, and ride bicycles most places in spite of a multibillion-dollar fortune. Most of the wealth came from helping others grow rich and assisting businesses raise money in the stock market. Like Carnegie, Cooperman comes from a very humble beginning. Like Carnegie, he worked like a dog for much of his life, and even today spends hours a day managing his wealth. I've never met him but would like to.

He watches and manipulates his investments like fly fishermen fish. He works hard to catch fish, and rejoices in a really successful day, and then releases the fish; or in Cooperman's case, gives the money away. One of my passions is fly fishing. Cooperman sees his work like a sport that he dearly loves. He fishes for money. He, like Carnegie believes the key to upward financial mobility, especially to the disadvantaged, is education. And while the Coopermans contribute to hospitals, food banks, local trusts, and endow programs, their primary focus is on education issues.

They have committed to funding higher education institutions and programs to make it easier for students to afford education to the tune of hundreds of millions of dollars. Cooperman believes that 'the world isn't meant to be totally even.' He is a true believer in the concept of equal opportunity and puts his money in that direction. He and Toby have committed to give away 90 percent of their wealth to the causes they believe in. That will be literally, billions of dollars. How much depends on how successful the fisherman is in landing new wealth along the way."

I appreciated Melody's note taking as I talked.

"Unlike Carnegie, the Cooperman's take a beating from those who do not understand the American economic system, upward mobility and wealth," said Lisa typing on her laptop. "A Washington Post article noted some of the negative mail they receive:

'Billionaires shouldn't even exist in America.'

'One day, we're coming after all you with pitchforks.'

'Wake up moron. YOU and your insatiable greed are at the root of our biggest societal problems.'

Leon doesn't get it. The post article included his history. He was born poor, went to public schools, worked his way through college, worked 80 hours a week after that and lived frugally. He understands the wealth gap and is troubled by it and sees the solution as the same one he used to grow wealthy. The capitalist system will allow you to move up if you are prepared and work hard."

"You really believe this, don't you?" asked Melody, staring at Lisa. "The system still isn't fair."

Lisa was prepared for that comment. "You assume that the

pie we all share is finite. I have a contractor client, one of Rodger's friends, Dave, who tells a great story about that. 'Imagine an Easter egg hunt with a bunch of kids. The supply of eggs, like human imagination is unlimited. Generally, the older kids will be more adept at finding eggs than the young ones. A portion of the kids will be highly motivated and more exceptional at finding eggs than others. Many of the successful egg finders will re-hide some of their eggs for the smaller kids. Rather than employing their imagination, alertness, concentration, and hustle, some of the hunters will resort to simply following the successful hunters, picking up only what is missed. Their motivation for wealth, eggs, will turn to envy and their motivation will shift from finding eggs to acquiring some of those already found. The unmotivated, miss the instructions that pointed out that there was an unlimited supply of eggs. To them, like in the economy, they see the pie as finite with the slices cut smaller and smaller as more want a piece.'"

"And, about that equity thing? In 1920 there were about 12,000 millionaires in America, 6 of whom were Black. Today there are about 22,000,000 millionaires and 340,000 are Black. Not equal but a much better percentage. Millions more are other people of color. But the task before us is increasing overall income of American families, all families, **with no racial component**. Improvement will come from education, training, and growing the pie. It will come as more of us take responsibility for earning our own living, advancing, and achieving greater success. Not everyone in America has the ability to grow their wealth with as little effort as possible, but the vast majority do," replied Lisa.

I knew her story and smiled as she started to relate it.

"I started out working at McDonalds and five years ago my partner and I created a trust to provide work experience incentives for business to hire kids from the inner city to start them on their way. I studied in high school, started flipping burgers and waiting on customers. I took what I learned and went on to college, studying finance. Then I worked as a waitress while I studied to become a stockbroker. With every paycheck, I put a small amount into my investment portfolio, even when it meant that I ate ramen for dinner. I built a clientele and helped them with their investments and kept pushing my own until I could afford to leave it all behind. Today I use those same investment skills to grow the money people have committed to doing real good."

Lisa began to pull the half dozen pages spread out in front of her into a pile. "I've got another meeting in ten minutes," she said, "but I heard that you met with Barry Salazar the other day. I'm sure you heard his comment, **YOU OWN YOU.** If you will write that over and over, maybe you can help our especially disadvantaged kids believe it. Reminding kids that they are victims, that there are obstacles in front of them sends the wrong message. Obstacles are not barriers, if you own you and believe in yourself you will figure out how to jump over or walk through them."

"Is it reasonable to expect people to overcome obstacles on their own? Shouldn't we pay everybody a lot more?"

"Not paying people who aren't busting it is not a popular position for progressive thinkers. They either do not understand how business works or have an extremely misguided understanding of who makes what. In a 2021 survey of students at The Wharton School of the University of Pennsylvania, the majority believed that the average American wage was over $100,000 per year. In reality, the average wage in 2020, according to the Social Security Administration, was $53,383 and the median wage was $34,612. Among industries with the lowest profit margins is the restaurant business. When pushed to increase pay without productivity and profit, improvement the industry's solution is not positive for workers."

"I still think most people, especially public employees can't get their fair share. How do they succeed?" asked Melody as we waited for the elevator.

"Good question," I answered as we walked. "That's our next meeting."

4

MELODY MEETS ELLEN

WE STARTED OUR next meeting at the same coffee shop. I knew that Melody wouldn't have another article out for a couple of days and was curious as to how she might frame the meeting with Lisa.

"I get the ladder thing," she started. "Entry level, supervisor, innovator, manager, business owner and then put some of your money to work. My friends and I were talking and honestly, I couldn't explain the jump from entrepreneur to capitalist."

"An entrepreneur is just a businessperson who keeps on growing their business and often expands into new fields when they see opportunity, like Barry did when he started opening fast food outlets. A capitalist is someone who has put money away for some period, usually in the stock market or some real estate. At some point they have enough in their investments that their full-time job becomes managing their money. They invest in companies that they think will pay good dividends to their shareholders or in business ventures where they can make a small investment early and cash in as the business becomes very successful."

"Most people will never be able to afford that. That sounds really risky."

"It can be, and you might well lose your entire investment. But if you do really well on one investment it can made enough to cover losses in four or five other investments. But you are right, you might lose it all. It happens, but by the time most high money investors transition to managing their own portfolio, they have developed the skills to succeed. You would be surprised where some of the most successful investors come from."

Melody nodded but it was clear that she still wasn't sure that wealth, at least inherited wealth was a good thing. Not knowing where she would go next, I used that silence thing again.

"A lot of people today just are not getting the education to succeed. And even if you have a good idea, where would a poor kid get the money to start a business?"

"Our meeting today will be here in the coffee shop. Ellen will be a great one to discuss the education thing with. When we wrap up that meeting, I'll try to reach a friend on the phone. He is one of the best examples I know of why people do not have to stay in poverty. While we wait for Ellen to get here, let me give you my personal thought on where you get the money."

"Do you have another clever quotation for me?"

"Not yet. Do they bother you?

"Not really, in fact, I'm jotting them down to use in stories."

"Okay, here's a story. The two kids that founded United Parcel Service, the largest parcel delivery company in the world, founded the company for $100 about a hundred years ago in Seattle. They put their two bicycles to work delivering between business offices and grew the company into a worldwide powerhouse. To do the same thing today because of inflation you would need to raise about $3,000. Not simple, but completely achievable with a good idea, even if you can only approach family and friends."

About that time, a frail light skinned black woman with her head wrapped in a bandanna waived from the front door. I couldn't help but notice that my old friend Ellen looked terrible. I stood and helped her into a chair and started waived to the barista. "Can we have a double shot espresso here?"

"Rodger, how about a green tea instead," said Ellen. "The cancer medications I'm on are holding the cancer at bay, but they make coffee feel like pure acid in my stomach."

"Switch that order to a tall green tea, please," I called.

While we waited for Ellen's tea, I introduced her to Melody. "Ellen is a retired public-school administrator," I started. "She is my go-to for accurate information on education for my books. She's a bit of an outsider today since she is quite outspoken about where we are headed with education in this country. I asked her to join us today to explain how she built substantial wealth as a public employee, but I'm sure she would be happy to answer your concerns about why so many kids are not getting the education they deserve."

Ellen took a sip of her tea, and it was obvious that she was having trouble swallowing. Still, she smiled at Melody and opened with, "I am so happy to be here for a discussion with you. Let's get the money nonsense out of the way so that we can talk about education. Would that be okay with you?"

Melody nodded and set her recording phone on the table close to Ellen to capture her soft voice.

"I spent four years in the Army right out of high school. My single mom couldn't afford to help me with college, so she suggested the military to give me access to the GI Bill for college. I graduated in four years and began my teaching career when I was 26. I taught for sixteen years, using my summers for fun and for advancing my education. When I was 42, I took a summer and a year to get my master's degree in educational leadership and then spent twenty years as a principal and then assistant superintendent of a Chicago area school district." Ellen struggled through another sip of her tea.

"From day one, I was counting on the retirement program available to educators and with thirty-six years of service, retired with an income close to what a school principal earns plus health care and other benefits. But more importantly, I'd learned from my mom that you need to put a small amount away every month, so I did just that. It wasn't enough to really cramp my lifestyle, but by saving 5 percent or more of every check, on the day I retired, my broker had grown that into more than a million dollars. That gives me an extra $40,000 a year and I use it to promote educational reform."

I could tell that Melody was impressed. Hell, I'd been impressed since I first met Ellen eight years before, at a city council debate on arts and education funding. She had just lost her husband, but you would never have known that as she blasted the city for years of refusing to reform education. Dressed in black, this black woman was a powerhouse. She'd appeared in my sixth book as a former educator forced into an action role. The book was set in a country where she was guest teaching, and when civil war exploded, my Ellen-like character had no choice but to become a fighter to protect 'her kids." In the end, she paid with her life, and I always regretted killing her off, since she would have worked great in a couple of future books. Ellen loved the book.

Melody looked over at me with a sly smile. "I'd like to know how you knew that part of my upcoming story is about how public servants just don't have the same opportunity to grow wealth as people in the business world?"

"Honestly, I hadn't anticipated that, but I've watched Ellen put her money to work to support what was important to her and thought that might add to what Lisa told you about what wealth means to different people and how they use it."

Melody turned to Ellen. "So, just what in education needs to be fixed to make it fair to everybody?"

I could tell that just coming to this meeting was a chore for Ellen. I hadn't known about the cancer, and we'd talked only months before. But I also knew that anyone who could help her bring real reform to education would light up her day.

"First, and foremost, we haven't changed the public educational model since I was born in the 1950's. Can you think of anything else so important to society that just hasn't changed? Oh, there are multiple educational models available today. Besides public schools, you still have faith based and private schools, and today a lot of parents teach their kids at home. The private schools did really well during the recent pandemic because they kept the schools open and kids engaged. Home schooling works if a kid is lucky enough to have a parent who can devote the time to their lessons and growth. Generally, private schools and home schools aren't available for kids from poor families where even if the kid is lucky enough to have two parents at home, they are working all the time."

"I agree," offered Melody. "That was and is my real concern. These kids just don't have a chance."

"The overall performance of traditional public schools has been falling since President Carter created the Federal Department of Education, four decades ago. The majority of educators know something needs to change. Pay for great teachers is woefully inadequate. Pay for good teachers needs to increase. Poor teachers are already overpaid. Pay and performance should perhaps be linked. That is, if the obstacles to teacher success are removed. But pay is just one part of the puzzle. Another part is that kids today are so diverse.

I believe that the idea of a teacher faced with a classroom of kids from broadly diverse backgrounds, languages, and degrees of preparation in the name of equity does a disservice to the most prepared, those in the middle and those who need more help. In a classroom of thirty students, how can any teacher provide what each individual student really needs. The goal should be to provide each student who owns themselves with the best opportunity. Many schools speak to individual personalized learning and then ask their overburdened teachers to manage to that without adequate time. Teachers often work 50 hours a week, and new teachers more than 60. Many of the worst performing school systems in America are ones where the teachers are paid well, and the schools are funded. Why is it that the majority of religious schools remained open during the pandemic and why do their graduates consistently succeed? How would it help those students or any others if we slow them down? "

I wasn't quite sure what Melody thought of Ellen's discussion, but I noted that her lips were tight and her knuckles white as she gripped her pen. "What should the schools look like today?"

"People your age will have to figure that out, but here are some thoughts. What I would hope you come up with, would not be a one size fits all approach, but one that helps everyone advance at a pace that allows them to reach their potential. It would be one where parents are in control, and where children of parents who do not want or cannot exercise control get help. It would not be critical of religious or private education but would emphasize what they do best.

There are some great public schools in America, but there are also some who have settled for pumping kids in one end of a pipe and out the other, hoping something sticks along the way. The A, B, C, D, F, grading system has become the A, B system because it makes those who are failing uncomfortable and harms the school's image and funding. Pre-K education may help, especially for kids from households that do not or cannot offer quality preparation for school. But for those kids who are prepared, why waste the money? Why bore prepared kids with lessons they already have mastered?"

"I need to think about that before I try to write about it," said Melody. "What you suggest seems really complicated and very expensive. Schools all over the country are having trouble with budgets."

"What is clear is that the parents are deciding that they own themselves, and they own the responsibility for their children and the 100-year-old model for America's public schools is not one they have confidence in. It is only a matter of time until they put their pocketbooks where their heart is. Nationwide, school budgets now exceed what it costs to run the entire government of local communities, fire, police, water, everything.

The concept that academic advancement be guided by age is obsolete. Advancement for students and faculty must be guided by performance. The transition might be tough, after all we have become so sensitized to how others feel that we really struggle to hurt their feelings, even if that is what is needed to help them succeed. We need to find a way to replace actions based on feelings with plans based on thinking."

"I'm having trouble with that," replied Melody. "Kids, especially middle school age kids and high schoolers are really influenced by their peers and how they are perceived."

"Ellen and I have talked about this a lot," I offered. "Just because it will be difficult is no reason not to figure this out. Overcoming these tropes isn't new. For those who are old enough and attended school in areas where migrant families worked in agricultural fields, one remarkable thing became obvious. Children of these families who moved regularly seldom had an opportunity to complete more than a few months of school in any one place. But the education they received was treasured. Watching a twelve-year-old boy engaging with eight-year-old kids in the third grade was an eye opener.

They knew they were different, and at a different level. They saw most of their twelve-year-old peers in the seventh grade. But they were hungry to learn and take school seriously. Unfortunately, you seldom see this anymore. If a twelve-year-old kid performs at a third-grade level, we need to accommodate them and quit stigmatizing them or placing them in classes where they grow frustrated and quit. Or even worse, advance them along with kids their age even if they haven't mastered what the school tried to teach them."

"And there is the challenge," offered Ellen. "We need to change the view of education among that part of the population that doesn't treasure it. If the parents can't do that, then we need to adjust the schools themselves to make education more important than anything else."

Ellen smiled at me and then at Melody. "My docs tell me that I only have a few more months to live. Right now, I'm working to figure out how I leave what I have to help implement my educational dreams. Both my kids are successful. They don't need the money. But they tend to believe that education reform is really critical. I just need to come up with a plan to put what I have to work."

Melody beat me to it. "We just had a meeting with Lisa Renfro, and she was talking about setting up trusts for people who wanted to leave their wealth to causes they care about. Maybe she can help."

"I hadn't thought about Lisa and her group," replied Ellen, "Great idea. If this works out, you'll have some reason to think about me when I'm gone."

"Ellen, for now I'm not ready to start thinking about that. You're still here, and still the Ellen I've known most of a decade," I offered.

About that time, the door to the shop opened and a late thirty-ish dark-skinned woman dressed like a teacher looked over at us and then headed to the counter to order.

"There's my ride," said Ellen. "Cynthia is really shy. She's between classes so I'd better run. I'm helping her with picking a school for her master's in education."

We watched as the newcomer held the door for Ellen and as the older woman struggled to get into the back seat of a Prius with an Uber sticker on the window.

"That's what I mean," said Melody. "That woman is teaching and driving for Uber and about to begin work on a master's degree. It's not reasonable, something has to give."

"Oh," I replied. I waited for a response for more than a minute before I picked up my phone. Melody just sat.

"We're calling my friend John. He's a great example of success. He's from East St Louis and grew up with a mom who was a nurse's aide. He lost his father at a young age. His stepfather worked in Civil Service. Combined, the family never made twenty-five thousand dollars in a year. Not much to support a family of seven. The neighborhood is the poorest in America, the population is almost all Black, and filled with examples of failure. Reporters write that people there 'just don't have a chance.'"

John answered on the first ring. After explaining what Melody and I were exploring, he began as if he'd known Melody for years.

"My parents struggled to overcome community influences with their faith-based messages. I grew up in East St Louis, the poorest city in the country, a lot of crime and poverty.

I refused to be sucked in. My mom really supported me. I did a work study program at my high school, qualifying by entrance exam. Only 15 percent of the mixed-race pool of applicants were admitted to the program. I'd crammed for weeks before the exam. The job, working around blue collar workers and management in an auto parts company showed me success. Entry workers who worked hard and intelligently moved up. Those same workers encouraged me. They managed their lives and looked to the future.

I took the $700 I'd saved and applied to a state university. My stepfather told me I was nuts, that I was wasting money. Later, I used some grant money and continued working part time to graduate. Nothing was going to stop me.

Next, I joined the Air Force as an intelligence officer and later was a successful sales manager for a national life insurance company. At every step, people discussed obstacles and at every step I saw only the next opportunity. I still see only the next opportunity. Not all of my siblings have been as successful. I have a sister who became a doctor and another a successful educator. I have a brother who can't seem to stay out of jail. I saw only hurdles while he spent his early years stymied by perceived obstacles. A lot of my friends followed his path."

"Do you believe that others from a similar background can do the same?" asked Melody.

"Only if we quit trying to convince kids from my kind of background that they are victims," replied John. "I'm a person of faith and am just frustrated that even some churches have bought into the victim forever thing. But the fastest way to get your house burned down in the old neighborhood is to openly challenge that idea; to bluntly tell the community that it's up to them to succeed on their own. Poverty is now a business and generates a lot of money."

"Any questions for John?' I asked.

"I don't think so," replied Melody. "Oh, one. What do you do now?"

"I volunteer a lot and dabble in investments; I've made a bundle and lost a bundle in crypto currency in the last five years. I limit what I put on the table, and do my homework, never risking our retirement or the money my wife and I use to do good work. If there is nothing else, I've got a golf date in an hour." And with that, he was gone.

"How many people like John are there?" asked Melody.

"I think he is in the majority, but he's not one of the squeaky wheels you write about."

I watched Melody's face and body language, thinking she was about to challenge that.

"Let's skip the last couple of questions about the economy for now. I'd like to skip to my questions on social justice."

"Okay," I replied. "You'll need to give me something more specific."

"I've got an editorial meeting this afternoon. I'll call tomorrow. Thanks for introducing me to your friends. I'm not sure that any of this is changing how I feel, but thanks."

"Don't ever abandon your concerns and feelings. Maybe, rethink what to do about them. But it's never wrong to care about your fellow man."

5

EDITORIAL MEETING

THE EDITORIAL COMMITTEE consisted of the publisher, editor, two division managers and two public members. The meeting started with a big vote of confidence in Melody's first story on the economy. All agreed that she nailed how the employee, employer system works. Her editor who had reviewed a first draft of the second story on wealth, opened a discussion of that story among the group.

"It's not the story that we expected," he started, "but it does explain why conservatives support the existing system. Melody's piece includes some interviews that surprised me. You also read the draft. Naomi, your thoughts?"

Naomi Becka, leaned across the table, fixing Melody with a stare. "I was there when Melody met this guy who is guiding her through her research. I'm not sure how reliable a source you meet in a bar is. I have a boat load of colleagues all over the country who have spent a lifetime studying economics and social justice issues. Any one of them might offer a more studied discussion. I always cringe when John Q. Public is portrayed as the expert rather than academics and other intellectuals who devote their lives to exploration and policy."

"That was to be the focus of the series," replied the editor. "We were trying to figure out what the conservative movement appeal was. I think we all want to see real change, but if we only reach out to people who think like us, it will never happen."

Dr. Becka tapped on a few keys on her laptop. "I pulled together some thoughts last night. Here are some questions. Why do they cling to a two-hundred-year-old document, created only by white men, when society has evolved past most of the issues from that period? Second, how can anybody not see that the current system ignores social justice and the obvious answers to improving it and why, when judges rule that system is unfair is that not accepted? Third, much of the social justice crises are rooted in a lack of economic justice, and Melody's first story only parrots what conservative media has said for years instead of finding real solutions. Finally, how can anyone today claim that liberty is more important than equality, and society's responsibility to achieve economic and social justice? We all know how the system is today, we need to be figuring out how to fix it. Until the last couple of decades, even conservatives relied on the advice of people like me, who, in spite of being horridly underpaid, devoted our lives to research on how to make all lives better, not some lay person who only thinks about these things when they have a break from trying to make a buck."

The publisher, who up until that moment had remained quiet, smiled. "Dr. Becka, you and I have spent years discussing the failures of society. Those are all pertinent questions, and need to be tacked onto Melody's next story, which is probably a bit too supportive of how things are today. Still, our intent was to reach across the aisle with this series."

Turning to Melody, he asked, "Can your contact help dig into the other side's thoughts on these questions?"

"I'll send him a revised set of questions this afternoon." Turning to Dr. Becka, she continued, "But I've tapped into a whole set of people who are giving us just what we started out to find and I'm not going to ignore what they are telling me."

"Melody, the other side really thinks we are incorrect. You can't get manipulated into justifying beliefs that are just plain wrong. You can be part of ending this evil."

6

WHERE TO FROM HERE?

I LIKED THE second story on wealth, as well. Melody had presented the insights from our last couple of meetings. I recognized that her passion for DEI issues still drove her reporting, but the summary of the second story laid the groundwork for some middle ground.

So, to this reporter, the four pillars of our current economic system make sense. Get started on a job where you can learn, work hard, and climb the success ladder. On your way up, recognize that you will be supporting those further up the ladder and helping those below. You can be an entrepreneur, a business owner, or a capitalist if you are innovative and committed. Once you arrive, once you have wealth, you might well find more joy in giving back than in owning.

The preview for the rest of the series was a bit more concerning. *The system works for many, but not for all of us. In the following stories we will explore how a system designed to grow the wealth of all, leave families of color with only a fraction of the wealth of white families.*

That was concerning to me, not because of the answers, but because I considered that the people who I would introduce Melody to would offer answers that would conflict with her feelings. That was on my mind as we met for coffee the following morning. We agreed to begin with Melody interviewing me. I had just finished a draft of a book that included this issue.

"Allow me to paraphrase your questions to make sure that I understand them so that I can connect you with people who offer answers," I started.

Melody seemed a little uneasy, but nodded as she stared into her laptop at the note she'd sent me a couple of days before.

"First, why do we follow a constitution written two centuries ago when slavery ruled America, a document obviously created exclusively by white men, many of whom were slave owners? America only rebelled when Britain moved to outlaw slavery. Hasn't society evolved?

Second, there is obvious inequality in America. Why are policies and legal decisions addressing those inequalities overturned by others who refuse to see the failures of the constitution?

Third, social justice problems are rooted in economic inequality, and in 200 years we have not been able to overcome that inequity.

Finally, you want to understand which comes first, equality or freedom. What is the relationship between equity and liberty? How can anybody who feels unequal ever be truly liberated?

Allow me to add a final area of exploration. I suspect we differ on rights versus obligations, and both are influenced by the relationship of privileges versus responsibilities.

Melody, to adequately cover all of this, we need to review thousands of years of history, the entire foundation of the legal system, and what has happened since the first pilgrims came to America. Are you up for this?"

"You offered to help me with this project. If it is too much, I can try to find another source."

Something or someone had changed Melody's interview strategy.

"I'm not backing away from this. Hell, I write historical fiction and most of what I write is based on just these issues. The challenge will be to find colleagues willing to spend the time to answer your questions who will also be willing to cut off an interview after they do. Most of the engaged people I know won't shut up once they get started."

"Then let's start with what you think, Rodger. You spend months every year doing research," replied Melody. "You wrote a book about racism in World War II, so let's start there."

She had her phone out, ready to record, but showed no in indication of taking notes.

"Okay, here goes. There are a lot of folks who look at American society and the economy today and see problems. They feel that the problems are institutional and because of that, the institutions need to be torn down. Okay, I understand how they feel, but I challenge you to think in addition to feel.

American society is a long way from perfect. But it doesn't take a deep dive to arrive at alternatives to tearing it down. First, you would have to ignore almost 250 years of progress…not perfection but progress. Second, you would have to understand that there are no historical examples of anything better. Let's start with racism."

I waited for Melody to look up, but she seemed focused on her latte. I needed to start somewhere that would get her attention. **"Racism seems to be the justification for a lot of complaints about America,"** I started in a voice that carried across the room. She looked up and smiled. It was the smile of someone who knew they held a winning hand.

"In a way, the United States didn't have a chance to avoid racism. Race was a seldom used concept in Europe through the 1500s. It was a term that separated people by geographic origin, sometimes by religious affiliation, and by characteristics, nothing to do with slavery.

By the 1600s European elites and philosophers were developing what they believed were "scientific" laws that allowed society to separate people by race, which in that period almost always included skin color. These scientific laws looked at head shape, cultural advancement, technological development, written language and other traits and customs. These weren't the laws of nature, but rather, laws about nature drawn from prejudiced observation. They were portrayed as facts much the same as early religious beliefs were portrayed as facts.

Those philosophers declared that white skinned people were superior to those of other skin colors. That because of their "superior" intelligence, culture, and religions they should be the dominant race. Tragically, this was accepted almost all over the world. People of color, who were being subjugated and defeated in warfare by superior European technology in their own lands, were forced to accept that they could not compete. They did not acknowledge that they were less as human beings, only that they could not protect their lands, families, religions, and culture from technically advanced armies. Many, for their cultures to survive, accepted European dominance, even in the Americas.

By the early 1600s it was widely accepted that Africans, captured by other Africans, often brokered by Arabs, were inferior to the point that they could be enslaved as workers. It was a lot less effort to force inferior people to work in the fields than do it yourself.

Slavery itself is as old as organized civilization. Up until the 1600s slaves were not defined by race, only by military might. Perhaps 4,000 years of slavery preceded the creation of the United States. The Romans practiced slavery. Russia and the Slavic states had centuries of slavery history as did the Crimea and the Barbary Coast of Africa. Christian, Ottoman, and Islamic nations practiced slavery. Slavery was even part of what some societies called blood tax, where children were taken from parents and sold into slavery because the parents could not pay their taxes. Asian societies practiced slavery, again with most slaves captured in warfare. No one cared what color a slave's skin was.

African and American indigenous groups captured people from other tribes and put them to work. All would work or starve. In the seventeenth and eighteenth centuries, more than 300,000 white people were shipped to America as slaves. Some were criminals, others street urchins, some were duped into becoming indentured servants, unaware that once in the new world they could be bought and sold as property. The first people sent to colonize Australia were white criminal slaves.

Slave labor was cheap and helped a lot of people all over the world, from many ethnic groups, improve their family wealth with a lot less effort than doing it themselves. **Remember, that before capitalism, the only path to wealth was to steal it or enslave others to work for you.** Capitalism was one of the essential processes that eventually made slavery obsolete, by unchaining the power of innovation especially in technology. That didn't happen overnight.

But race became a clear delineator of slavery in the new world. And one thing was universal of all slaves, they did **not own** themselves. Never forget Salazar's comment, you own you, your time and the wealth produced with that time. But not for a slave and it didn't mean that they accepted their fate. Slaves were a lot of trouble, always a threat. Slave rebellions in southern states spilled both black and white blood. The carnage of the slave rebellion in Haiti, which ended with the nation's independence from France in 1803 shocked and terrified the American South.

Slaves supplied the manpower for much of the economic expansion of the early Americas. I remember an economics professor, desperate to find a justification for his feelings that slavery was never economical. The fact is, that slaves were the tractors, the graders, the hay rakes, cotton planters and harvesters, the grain combines of American economic expansion. They built buildings, they used picks and shovels to create roads. Slavery was not only economically justified; it was critically important to the early economic success of America, and across the globe.

Slaves were especially valuable in agriculture where they could not only tend crops, but also grow enough to feed themselves. Imagine your John Deere tractor creating all the fuel it uses. By the 1800s, the number of slaves in the Caribbean states had grown so much that food crops grown around the sugar plantations could not support the population. New England's salted fish industry exploded due to the demand from Caribbean countries that had to keep their slaves from starving. Even abolitionist New Englanders participated, arguing that if they did not, a lot of people would starve.

In some cases, the slaves employed by an enterprise were worth more than the real estate where they worked. But throughout the early history of the Americas there was also a strong movement to end slavery.

As you noted in our phone call, there is a great deal of discussion now over slavery being the catalyst for the American Revolution. The 1619 project of the New York Times argues that that Americans only revolted from England because the English were about to abolish slavery. This seems to be a conclusion in search of a factual argument. The English parliament didn't even begin debating the elimination of slavery for two decades after the American Revolution. By the time the American Civil War broke out, there were about 4 million slaves, most of them Black, helping people grow wealth in America. Very few were recent arrivals from Africa.

Anyone who believes that men naturally want to create more wealth can understand that a single man with a hoe can work a lot less land than a man with slaves helping. Slavery was practiced for about 230 of the 500 years after the first Europeans came to the new world. No one really knows how long the original native people used the practice.

Slavery ended in America 166 years ago, that is just over five historical generations. Some are of the opinion that America must compensate the victims of slavery. The number of black people has grown from 4 million to 41 million in those 166 years. One of my favorite stories is from the second year after the end of the Civil War. A plantation owner begged his former top slave to come back and work for him. The slave sent him a bill for 22 years of past wages with a note that he would consider it after payment was received. The request from a former slave makes a lot of sense. Compensation to his great, great, great granddaughter is more questionable. It may make some people feel better, but it is nonsense.

Melody interrupted. "Since the time of slavery, black people have suffered. Their wealth is a fraction of white wealth. It started with slavery, so why doesn't society owe their heirs?"

"Melody, between 1865 and 2006, the Federal Government passed 14 major civil rights acts and constitutional amendments, one per decade. Perhaps we can change the perception of slavery. Not the one that makes it clear that it was wrong and an abomination. No, the one where decedents of slaves somehow still feel shame, they too are victims. The black slaves who worked without compensation, suffering abuse and humiliation through the mid 1800s were critical to building the foundation of the country. Their resourcefulness and **resilience** in the face of horrid conditions is, at least to me, a really uplifting part of our history. The nation needs to clearly applaud the efforts, resilience, and contribution of its first black members. Only in the last couple of decades are the stories of the rebels among the slaves being told. Any critical examination of historical documents reveals this nation's extraordinary efforts to heal the wounds of slavery. It also will shine a spotlight on the nation's failures. But society has invested 22 trillion dollars over the last 50 years to remedy the problem, about a million dollars for every black citizen alive in 1970; you know the results."

"You still haven't explained how the 1619 project was wrong."

"Okay, so what fueled the revolution against the British if it wasn't slavery? For two and a half centuries historians studying the papers of the founding fathers wrote that it all boiled down to "you don't own me." I paused before adding, "that keeps coming up."

"Thomas Paine was a Brit, a writer, who came to America at the invitation of Ben Franklin. He was a social revolutionary in England and brought his beliefs with him. His book COMMON SENSE came out as tensions rose between the colonists and England. It became one of the most widely read books in the world and is credited with sparking citizen revolution against oppressive monarchy in America and across Europe and the globe. In many places slavery wasn't an issue where COMMON SENSE helped drive rebellion.

There were real differences between the Americans and their British masters, even though colonists were supposedly British citizens. Most differences were centered around taxes imposed by the British government on the colonies. Britain had been engaged in extensive warfare for years and pressed the colonists for the money to help pay off the Crown's debts. The colonies were prohibited from electing their own governors. British law treated the colonists as lesser citizens. British soldiers bullied and humiliated Americans. Americans were prohibited from manufacturing goods that real English citizens made and wanted to sell to the colonies. While people in England were steadily stripping power over their lives from the King, the government they created worked with the King to hold down colonists' ambitions and dreams.

Eventually the discourse devolved into protest and civil disobedience. We all know about the BOSTON TEA PARTY. Americans objected to the Crown's rules that made England the only country that the Americans could trade with. The citizens refused to comply. The British monarch responded by sending troops into the streets of Boston, forcing the citizens to house, and feed the soldiers in their own homes. A majority of the citizens just wanted to remedy the Monarch's injustices. They were okay with remaining British citizens. But the government began a campaign of repression that just inflamed the people. No one really knew what to do. Attempts to negotiate with the government were failing. All attempts to appeal to the King were rebuffed."

Melody finished her coffee and waived for another. Three strong coffees and I would be in and out of the restroom every fifteen minutes. Her coffee arrived, as she closed her laptop.

"Thomas Paine's COMMON SENSE made four arguments for independence." I handed Melody a copy of the argument from my research binder, and she began to read.

1. *The history of mankind:*
    Individual men, isolated, independent, free, create free societies as they form more complex government. Without checks and balances those governments often develop anti-social elements and policies. Those governments become what many consider a necessary evil, and sometimes an intolerable evil.
2. *Anti-monarchy:*
    There is no logical, biological, or moral right to hereditary leadership. Societies create leaders to coordinate their efforts and safety. You follow a leader for three reasons:
    - *You fear them (monarchy)*
    - *You follow their intellect (enlightened)*
    - *Your life or livelihood depends on them*
    When leaders no longer make life better, or worse threaten it, society has a right to change them.

3. *Focus on the colonies and their societies:*
    - *The break with England is inevitable and justified.*
    - *Independence is a shield against corrupt or antagonistic foreign monarchs or governments.*
    - *Separation allows each of the 13 colonies to emphasize their strengths while allowing America to become a trading hub to the world without foreign entanglements; and*
    - *Separation opens the door to freedom loving refugees in an empty land.*

4. *To succeed in a rebellion against England, the rest of the world needed to see and understand the injustices and to believe that America intended to win its independence. The people needed to advertise their clear intent and goal and that would open the door to foreign help and recognition. They needed a plan.*

"If the American public had seen any progress toward reconciling the injustices they felt, the American Revolution would not have happened, at least not at that time. But nothing got better, and the King cracked down."

"Hold it, the land wasn't empty, it was full of Indigenous people," said Melody.

"Remember that this was the 1770s and 'educated' people believed that white people were superior and as such, the Native American's inefficient use of land was wasteful. This is history and as such is not for any of us to like, or even dislike, but to understand and learn from. History is not open to revision.

Paine's arguments refer to "natural laws" which at the time were a combination of actual biological/physical laws and the teachings of the Christian Church. These Americans believed that they had natural rights to grow their wealth and take care of their families. They lived in a time that allowed many to use the labors of others without paying for their time through the institution of slavery. But only a small percentage of citizens owned slaves. Many of their peers were working to end the practice. All were willing to risk everything to poke the King in the eye and snarl, **you don't own me.**

So, Paine's arguments led perhaps a third of the population to favor separation from England. Perhaps another 20 percent would never agree to separation and the remaining population took a wait and see attitude. Once hostilities began, those opposing separation supported the English, actually joining their military efforts. Many of those in the middle eventually supported the cause of independence.

The Declaration of Independence was signed by 56 men. At that time the society granted almost all governmental power to men. Forty-one owned slaves, but there were also ardent abolitionists. Twenty-three were lawyers, eleven were merchants, many were farmers or plantation owners, all were educated. None were Black or Native American, but that does not make them stupid or wrong. Their focus was on mankind.

Some were captured by the British and tortured, some died, almost all lost all or part of their families. Of the 56, only 13 maintained their wealth and lives. Many eventually died penniless.

The founders knew the risk when they signed and many paid a terrible price, but the survivors and their peers went on to create the United States of America and to write a constitution that is a model for the world, and a process for modifying the Constitution that has been used 27 times. Among the initial amendments were those that created what we know as the Bill of Rights. Few other nations, including England, have anything like it. The American society has used the amendment process to address issues never considered by the founding fathers and to alter their original intent as society changed. Today liberal thinkers, growing frustrated that they cannot get congress to enact policies they favor, because the

Constitution does not support those positions, have pushed for reformist judges who reinterpret the Constitution or simply argue that it does not apply.

The fact that the rules that we live by cannot be easily changed because some in the society have strong feelings is one of its greatest strengths. The founders wanted a set of rules that, unlike the laws of England, were not subject to the whims of the powerful. If society really wants change, they must convince the majority of the citizens in the states to amend the constitution. If you consider yourself 'enlightened' that process is tedious.

The American Revolution was not fought over slavery. It was, however, a clear starting point for the government recognizing that natural law gives us the right to build our wealth, including the acquisition of property through work. It was also the clear starting point for recognition that a European monarch did not own the American people and laid the groundwork that American people do not own other American people no matter what color they are. Between the adoption of the U.S. Constitution in 1789 and 1820, Congress passed five major anti-slavery acts, including the insertion of language in the 1820 Missouri Compromise that would end slavery. What everyone learned is that government legislation does not change the hearts and minds of the citizens. American independence requires the government to make a case and then the people can agree or disagree, as long as they understand there may be a price. Government cannot dictate what is in your heart.

Many in the South realized that the plantation economy depended on cheap labor and there was no less expensive labor than slavery. The South claims that the Civil War was fought over states' rights, while most northerners believe that it was about slavery. In the South, at that time, the two issues merged. They believed northerners didn't have the right to destroy them.

Many leaders of the southern states had been opposed to the

creation of a strong central government, fearing interference with their personal lives, livelihood, and local or state government. The Bill of Rights was added to the Constitution as a compromise to those who feared that a strong central government might run roughshod over its citizens. The very Bill of Rights that provides legal precedence for racial justice was, paradoxically championed by southern politicians. For many who owned slaves as beasts of burden it was a real stretch to look at those beasts as equal human beings. Yet the country had legislated from the 1820s forward, that slavery would be abolished. Southerners saw no replacement for slavery. The Civil War became inevitable."

"But, especially in the South, the rights of black people were still secondary to whites," observed Melody.

"The thirteenth amendment to the Constitution freed the slaves in the North as well as the South and gave them some basic rights. What the end of the war also did, was crush the economy of the South. Many southerners' entire net worth was in slaves. The plantations could not plant or harvest without workers. Many southerners had developed close relationships with slaves, but a lot of them still saw slaves as beasts of burden, not fellow citizens. Poor southern white people, and there were a lot of them after the war decimated southern industry, saw the newly freed black people as low-cost labor that would replace them in their already starvation wage jobs. Throughout the years of the war, the southern economy shrunk by as much as 80 percent.

The only people in the South, at the end of the war, who could build their wealth were northerners who took advantage of the desperate economy in the South by buying properties from destitute owners. Where that didn't work, they helped former slaves become political leaders in their communities. Former rebels were prevented from holding office. These black legislators, protected by federal troops, orchestrated tax increases on already stretched landowners. Northern carpetbaggers bought up properties as they were sold for unpaid taxes.

To many in the north, nothing was too terrible for the defeated South. To others, who took the longer view that the nation needed to heal its divide, such practices were abhorrent. For those today who believe that anyone remotely connected to historical slavery should be erased, imagine if the post-Civil War days were managed by people who believed that. We might still be fighting a guerilla war a century and a half later. The vast majority of southern leaders, people like Lee, supported reconciliation, including with Blacks. I would struggle to name any historical leader who had no flaws, made no major mistakes.

Blacks began to succeed in the former southern states. Some southern elites still considered them lower class humans but could do little to block their advancement because of tens of thousands of federal troops patrolling the South. Initially, several states sent black representatives to congress, all Republicans, assisted by a constitutional amendment that made former rebels unable to run for office. Even those southerners who had renounced the rebellion and worked with northern appointed officials toward reconstruction and human rights for freed slaves couldn't run for office. A decade after the war, most white southerners, while not supporting the causes of the rebellion, also didn't support Northern occupation. Southern life became showing the north that it didn't own them.

Over the next decade, the policy against white southern leadership in office eroded and the old-line Democratic Party slowly reemerged. With their return to power, those opposed to equal rights for freed slaves emerged, most notable, the Ku Klux Klan or KKK. As the North pushed for integration of new black citizens into the society, those who were still bitter over losing the Civil War and their treatment in the early days of reconstruction pushed back. By the election of 1876, the nation stood at the doorstep of a second civil war.

That election pitted Republican Rutherford B. Hayes against Democrat Samuel Tilden, and because of tainted voting tabulations in five states, neither could muster a majority of votes. The Republicans had controlled the Federal Government for almost a quarter century, and the Democrats, mostly southern, felt that the North was still running their lives through military presence. Eventually, a compromise was reached. Enough votes were awarded to Hayes for the Republican to become president while Hayes and the Republicans agreed to remove all troops from the South.

Over the next 80 years, freed slaves improved their lives, both through new lives in the North and by persisting under difficult circumstances in the South. In many northern states, they achieved equal status in citizenship, including running for office and voting. The South, still chaffing from their failure and humiliation during reconstruction, enacted laws that severely limited black citizens access to office and voting rights. Many, especially poor white citizens, reacted to black economic success with jealousy and envy, believing that much of that success had only come from the North, tilting the scales in favor of former slaves. Many of these same restrictions were extended to other groups, like American Indians. Disgruntled southerners with no economic stake in the South, spread into newly developing western territories. Many brought their attitude about race with them. Northerners in the same territories remained abolitionists.

Life for former slaves was better. **You don't own me** was better than being a slave.

Legislation did not change people's feelings, that would take time and a change of heart."

Melody sat quietly as I finally shut up.

"I guess I'm one of those people I talked about who can't quit talking," I offered, taking a sip of my stone-cold coffee.

"You just went a half-hour without coming up for air," said Melody. "You really do study this stuff, and you're not a professor or attorney. How do you remember all of that?"

"I just got on a roll. I wanted to address the first two questions you asked. And to me this is very important. It is the foundation of our economy, our society, and our laws. Let me add one final thought. You want to know why the constitution should govern the laws of the land. Let me ask you, if that document as amended by the people doesn't control our laws, who or what should? Should it be academics with little connection to common men and women? Even constitutional amendments are reversed. Remember people's views change all the time and even supreme court decisions are subject to review based on constitutionality. Dozens have been reversed. There was a decision that black people were not citizens. There was one that outlawed alcohol sales. Both were based on feelings and were overturned by justices who went back to the constitution."

Melody took a deep breath and shook her head. She paused before adding, "All that history is well and good, but people today are more enlightened, they have evolved and think differently."

"Ready for one of my quotations?" I asked opening my notebook. "The Roman statesman and philosopher, Marcus Tullius Cicero once observed the six mistakes man keeps making:

Believing that personal gain is made by crushing others.

Worrying about things that cannot be changed or corrected.

Insisting a thing is impossible because we cannot accomplish it.

Refusing to set aside trivial preferences.

Neglecting development and refinement of the mind.

Attempting to compel others to believe and live as we do.

Cicero died on December 7th, 43BC, more than 2,000 years ago and he was speaking of the preceding centuries. It is amazing how little man has changed, yet each generation seeks to see itself as more enlightened.

Melody looked a bit frustrated. She took quite a while before asking, "Where do we go from here?"

7

MELODY MEETS RETIRED JUDGE WILLIAMS

WE MET MY old friend Judge Williams where he and I often met, at a park overlooking the river. "Melody, Judge Williams was a history professor before turning to law. I thought he might be a really good source to discuss the debate over whether policy or the constitution should govern legal matters."

"I'm familiar with some of his decisions," she started. Most I agree with, but not all."

"I feel much the same about most of your bylines, Miss," replied the judge. "Some of which seem a little cumbersome from overthinking basic concepts. So, I'll keep this simple."

Melody leaned back on the bench where she was seated. "That statement seems like the opening of one of your decisions. I wouldn't expect anything else."

"First, a little bit about my background. I was and still am a Democrat. In the 1970's I was an anti-war activist and my first experience with the law was an arrest for a very vocal protest on my campus. My court appointed lawyer got the charges thrown out, based on my constitutional right of free speech. That experience is what drew me toward law school."

Judge Williams leaned back in his chair. "I really understand your passion. Four decades ago, I set out to change the world. I was going to use the legal system to right every wrong in America. What I learned, is that will never happen, if for no other reason, than what is considered right today, may not be in the future. I learned that solving one problem often created another, and that is not progress. Finally, I came to believe that we needed rules so that laws to help some didn't hurt the rights of others. Those beliefs came as much from historical study as from legal issues.

Much of the legal collision between what the media calls strict constitutional jurists and more liberal judges began in the early 1900s with the election of Woodrow Wilson to the presidency. Wilson was a self-declared progressive who pushed through a very aggressive list of bills to assert the power of the Federal Government over industry and the states. These included important laws such as those addressing child labor and the creation of the Federal Reserve. It also included several bills that tore responsibilities from the states and redeposited them with the Federal Government. Wilson saw the nation as one big pot of similar, if not identical culture, and the Federal Government as the policeman assuring that everyone did what they were told. The problem was that Wilson and his tiny group of advisors failed to see the differences across the land and picked winners and losers. Much of his decision making was based on the color of people's skin.

Many of the bills he pushed through Congress were questionable under our Constitution, but Wilson, as former president of Princeton University, Governor of New Jersey, and the only president who had a PhD, aggressively pushed judges, especially those he appointed to reinterpret the Constitution to allow legislation that addressed what he believed were critical societal needs. From that time on, groups like the current liberal legal think tank, **Demand Justice** have argued that policy is just as critical as law. They argue that broad interpretation of the intentions and goals, not just the actual words of the Constitution, should be the basis of legal opinion.

One of the critical responsibilities of the Constitution is to lay out a set of **principles** that guide the law and society. It also is supposed to protect against tyranny of either the majority or minority. Opening the words and intent of the Constitution to whatever interpretation elected officials find expedient takes away that principled guidance. President Wilson, the father of American Progressivism, was for example, a blatant anti-black racist. He used liberal legal interpretation, based on policy, to roll back the laws and rules of the reconstruction period, rules that opened the doors and offered opportunity to former slaves and their offspring. He went so far as honoring the KKK as he moved to repeal the anti-Klan legislation passed after the Civil War. The result was an almost total removal of black employees from the Federal Government and pressure for other government, social and business groups to do the same. Wilson saw black people as vastly inferior and considered it his duty to keep them away from the enlightened white people who elected him.

If Wilson really believed that the nation's primary codified law, the Constitution, needed revision, he had the amendment process available to him. But that takes years, and approval by the states, so it is more expedient to promote judges who think their beliefs allow them to reinterpret that document. Wilson, representing what he believed was a majority, almost single handedly demolished fifty years of social and economic justice for families of former slaves. He encouraged local anti-black activity from groups like the KKK. Other people of color were also singled out. I doubt that Wilson wanted to see them starve, but he surely did not want black Americans participating in government or the economy. This was in line with the Southern Democratic (Dixiecrat) policies followed since reconstruction. Black America's place in the economy was to provide menial labor. The majority can be more wrong than the minority.

As a progressive, Wilson also supported the Bolshevik Revolution in Russia. The new Communist government then betrayed his support by backing out of the war against Germany in World War I, collapsing the Eastern Front just as American troops were taking over the majority of fighting on the Western Front. The unintended consequences of his Bolsheviks' support cost the lives of thousands of American servicemen. The egalitarian utopia Wilson expected in Russia, was instead twisted to death by elected leaders Lenin and Joseph Stalin, who turned authoritarian. These enlightened leaders squashed all dissent in the name of equity.

Overly broad legal interpretations led to judicial decisions with substantial social impact. Wilson championed the idea that policy was equal to the Constitution in the courts. Many social driven legal decisions were overturned in the future, after years of suffering by those impacted. In 2022, the Supreme Court finally addressed the separation of church and state issues in the Constitution. Progressive thinkers, promoting the traditional idea of public education and secular private schools, have for decades made it illegal for government funds to go to religious schools. Even voucher programs provided to parents for educational support could not go to religious schools. Yet in many communities, the best schools were religious based and the majority of people who had access to them were middle- and upper-income families. But in the 2022 decision, the Supreme Court ruled that separation of Church and State was valid but could not discriminate against any school just because it was faith based. This opens the doors to some of America's best schools to people who could not otherwise afford them and raises the bar for the performance of all schools.

Since Wilson's term, some additional presidents have followed his model with the same consequences. Wilson's willingness to defy the Constitution set back the advancement of former slaves in the American economy like nothing else. It legitimized racism in political decision making. It also laid the groundwork for the courts and legislatures to impose huge burdens on individual citizens working to create wealth for their families and personal liberty. As President, he set in place laws and policies arguing that a minority of the nation's citizens didn't have a right to the American dream because they looked different and were therefore inferior."

Judge Williams stopped as quickly as he'd started. He watched both Melody and me but said nothing.

"So, you believe the courts are not the place to right society's wrongs," said Melody.

"It took a while, but yes," replied the judge. "The Constitution separates the government into three divisions, with different responsibilities. The court's job is to apply the laws of the legislative branch, arbitrate disagreements between government entities and people. It has no role in creating law, or even reinterpreting law outside of the intent of the legislative branch. Besides, the vast majority of social ills are best solved by the people themselves. If there isn't true buy-in to the goals of a law, then it will fail. The legal books are full of laws that accomplished little."

"But aren't we a democracy?" asked Melody.

"No, Melody, we are not. We are a republic of states founded on the word liberty. We use democratic elections to select the leaders of the republic. But the Republic's founding document demands liberty for each of its citizens."

"Okay, then, shouldn't we be a democracy, with the majority making decisions?"

"Ben Franklin once spoke to the power of liberty in a Constitutional Democracy, **'Democracy is two wolves and a lamb voting on what to have for lunch. Liberty is a well-armed lamb contesting the vote.'"**

As the judge headed out the door, I turned to Melody. "Tomorrow, I'd like to tackle the causes of economic inequality myself. Let's meet here again if that's all right with you. And then, I'd like to make a little field trip. I think it might help you write about equality and freedom, inequity, and liberty."

8

ALL THE BUZZ WORDS

I opened my notebook as Melody and I waited for our coffee. "I would like to begin our discussion of economic inequality with some facts rather than feelings," I offered.

Melody actually smiled as she responded. "I'm beginning to understand your focus on actions based on what you consider thinking versus actions based on feeling."

I didn't know if she really embraced that difference, but it was a focus of what I wanted her to understand, so I just dove in. "Over the last four decades the government has taxed producers, and even worse, borrowed money, trillions of dollars to compensate people to not participate in the most powerful economy on earth. While this paid some rent and put food on the table, it did little, except to pay them **not** to be part of the success. As manufacturing moved overseas and the rust belt grew, more and more people were paid just enough so that they would not fully take part in an economy that was going in new directions, in new locations, requiring new skills. Incredibly, the people pushing these payoff strategies have worked tirelessly to convince the recipients that they should support a government that pays them to survive instead of thrive. We all need to challenge this. Those affected should ask the question, **does government now own me? If you are substantially dependent on government, the answer may be yes.**

Government has not been very successful in helping people thrive.

What does this mean in real numbers, to real people? In 1960, twenty-two percent of Americans lived below the poverty level. Seventeen percent, or 30 million Whites were below the poverty level and 55 percent, or 10 million black Americans were considered impoverished based on numbers from the census bureau.

In 2020, America cut the poverty percentages in half, leaving only 11 percent of the population below the poverty level and 8 percent or 17 million white Americans fell into that category, while 19 percent or 8 million black Americans lived below the official poverty level.

In total numbers, it's important to consider that in the same period, the white population increased by 46 million or 29 percent. The black population increased by 22 million or 210 percent. White families had fewer children and white immigration was minimal. The black population increased through immigration with perhaps as many as 20 percent of the population new since the 1960's. Of greater impact, the number of black offspring increased by almost 100 percent. With no other factors, black family members dividing up inheritance would have received only about thirty cents of every dollar received by white family members. And, at the end of the slavery era, black families started with little or no wealth. What they accumulated was diluted by the enormous growth of black citizens.

Impoverished black citizens have decreased from 10 million to 8 million despite a more than doubling of the population, while white poverty has decreased from 30 million to 17 million in part to the stability of the population. Increased average black family wealth, over these 50 years, yielded much smaller pieces for black Americans than their white neighbors. Created family wealth was divided by more family members. But for both black and white Americans, there is another troubling factor.

I'm not criticizing family structure here. But you cannot ignore one statistic. In 1964, one-quarter of the country's black children and just over 3 percent of white children were born into single parent families. By 1990, that had increased to 64 percent of black children and 18 percent of white children. The opportunity to grow family wealth in a single parent household is diminished by perhaps as much as 80 percent in comparison to two family households. I was raised for most of my early life by a single mom. It was a financial bitch.

American institutions like banking, also contributed to black family poverty. For decades beginning with Woodrow Wilson's war on Blacks, they refused to treat black families the same as white. But that is one place where government regulation changed their behavior.

Today, with the war on energy, we are creating a new class of those left out. These are people in viable economic industries who are being pushed out of their jobs and the middle class because of politics. You wonder why so many blue-collar white people have become politically charged? Imagine being told that you are bad just because a job that may have supported a good living for generations is now politically incorrect. If you work in coal, you obviously hate the environment. Blue-collar white people see the majority of remedial programs pointed at the inner city and people of color and feel left out. They aren't demonstrating or rioting, and nobody is listening to them. Few even know that technology exists to reduce emissions from fossil fuels. Solar and wind energy may now be as much or more damaging.

There are still too many poor people in the country. In 2022, when the entire nation is screaming for employees, something other than government poverty programs is required. There are more jobs right now than people willing to work. Many in poverty would have to start at the bottom and then move up, but they are unwilling."

"Oh?" asked Melody. I loved her use of the old interviewer's trick to keep me talking.

"Yes, we need to quit paying people to survive and focus on preparing them to thrive through education and training."

"Oh, and how do we do that?"

"You've heard some good ideas in earlier interviews. The K-12 education system needs to make three fundamental changes. First, it needs to completely abandon social promotion and create curriculum that unleashes the power of those who are prepared, offering real remedial help to those who are not. Second, it needs to focus tax dollars on preparing citizen and legal immigrant children for success. There is room for assisting Dreamers in this policy, but we need to realize that it is diluting the education budget and infrastructure to be plugging students with 50 different base languages into the same classrooms as prepared students. Finally, we need to reject the educational elites' focus on college. We need to support the prepared and offer support to get the rest prepared. The idea of advancement based on your age needs to be replaced with advancement based on achievement."

"I don't believe that what you call the educated elites are against education in the trades," said Melody.

"Years ago, I participated in a forum on education. It was made up of about 60 percent local business executives, 20 percent people from non-profit programs and 20 percent from education. Of the 20 percent from education, perhaps two dozen were from the university environment. At the time I was representing a small airline and flight school. Along with dozens from trucking, heavy-construction communications and other business we came to plead the case for high school and initial years of college to refocus on preparing students for hands on jobs. A commercial pilot can be making over $200,000 annually within 10 years, and commercial truckers start in the range of $70,000, well above the average starting income of college grads, and we are desperately short of both pilots and truckers. The group put together a policy that made that type of preparation one of its foremost recommendations. At that point, several of the university people became incensed. One, a dean from a university stood up and chastised the group for being so shortsighted. I am paraphrasing here, but the gist of his comments went something like this. 'If you don't prepare students for a university education, including laying the groundwork for advanced degrees, you are failing them and the community and I for one will not add my name to such nonsense.'

That attitude included the process of hijacking parental responsibility to prepare children for life, the society, and the changing economy. The American educational system should include social concerns, but it needs to be secondary to offering knowledge and the ability to use that knowledge to make decisions. Refocus on core studies and encourage well educated academics and tradespeople, to use their own ability to think about their place in society and their responsibility to themselves, their family and fellow human.

What if the nation recreated manufacturing and other blue-collar industries including in the fossil fuel industry by abandoning the political correctness and sloganeering, offering real assistance to making industry as clean as possible with as much growth potential as possible? Today, a half-million pounds of mother earth is dug up to make a car battery which will last about 12 years before need to replace it with a new $20,000 electric battery. We need to accept that other than a rose, or a leaping rainbow trout, or perhaps a poem or two, there is no perfection in the world. There is progress, and every few years, some breakthrough changes the entire argument. Perfection is best left to deities beyond man and those they bless, with remarkable life and world changing ideas. You would never know it, but America's commitment to reduce pollution is succeeding. Auto pollution from fossil fuels is down by 80 percent.

History in the United Sates is one of consistent, measurable, and meaningful progress for all Natural Americans. We are a multi-racial, multi-cultural, multi-lingual society in a world that has struggled to avoid political problems by demanding conformity."

"You've used that term, Natural Americans in earlier conversations," commented Melody. "Where does that come from?"

"My friend Dave, the contractor. He's the first person I ever heard use that term. Let me dig out my notes, his words, from our first meeting." I opened my research binder and slid it over to Melody. Aloud she read from the first pages, a direct copy of Dave's comments to me.

> *"Chest puffed, feet spread, his five-year-old finger stabbing up toward the smirking face of his towering cousin, he snarled, YOU ARE NOT THE BOSS OF ME. Simple, resolute, and matter of fact.*
>
> *My boy was never taught this but there it was, a deep and thorough knowledge that he owned himself and he alone would determine what was in his best interest, at least until he crossed an out of bounds line that would lead to punishment.*
>
> *He was never given a menu to choose his own behavioral characteristics. That was done for him through generations of his ancestors, men and women who stuck their fingers in the face of kings and emperors, nobility, dictators and declared to them, YOU ARE NOT THE BOSS OF ME. Nobody had ever threatened him or encouraged fear of being his own boss.*

These are our ancestors, some already here and many more who came to America finding freedom. They left tribalism and feudalism behind seeking liberty. Freedom to worship as they saw fit and to own property, to prosper and be secure in the fruits of their own labor. Where no one else would be the boss of them they built the greatest nation in world history.

This is one of the precepts of how we might define a Natural American. A Natural American believes that he or she is an independent critical piece of what makes this country work. They believe that all they have to offer is their time (infusing time with their knowledge, critical thinking, and physical ability), and they alone own that time."

Melody stopped, her demeanor one of deep thought. "Does this apply to black Americans?"

"The creation of America was not smooth, I replied. In fact, it was more like dragging a wooden sled over a boulder field. Dozens of old beliefs, cultural and social institutions were discarded or destroyed. Bits and pieces of those same beliefs, culture and social institutions were molded together into a new society. Unfortunately, enslaved people, did not grow up poking their finger in the chests of others, crying, 'you don't own me.' Their ability and willingness to own themselves is a checkered tale. But throughout that history, they, like all Natural Americans, knew the truth. Blood was shed, traditions trampled, people fought and died. But eventually, the warring opponents became one nation, made up of diverse people. We can and should learn from our history and our mistakes, but you can never go back."

I wasn't sure that I'd succeeded in demonstrating to Melody that financial inequity was a very complex issue, one that defied simple slogans and answers. Perhaps, she still had questions, but she made it clear that she was ready to move on.

"You mentioned a field trip. One that you said might change my thoughts. Even with all we've discussed, I believe that equality is more important than liberty. Freedom means little without equality." She paused for a full minute. "I get your focus on responsibility, and personal responsibility and how it affects people's lives. Obligations come before any of us can secure our rights. But there is no greater privilege than equality."

"Pack up your stuff," I replied, "my old friend Chad Gritt has arranged for you to meet with some folks he works among."

Melody was obviously uncomfortable as we stopped at the fenced gate to the Pauch River Correctional Facility. She was more uncomfortable as Chad, the warden, greeted us in his office.

"Rodger called me and discussed the research you are doing. I follow your articles and commend you on both the quality and content of your writing. I'm happy to contribute to your last couple of stories."

Melody was overcoming her nervousness as Chad ushered us into a conference room where three inmates waited. All were trustees, and all had been at Pauch River for at least ten years.

The conversation began with Melody asking each why they were incarcerated. Then Chad asked them to describe an average day in prison. The discussion became more esoteric.

One of the inmates was Black, another Hispanic, and the third white. Each was obviously intelligent, and each found a way to make the pitch on how they had reformed and why they were good candidates for release. After a half hour, the warden excused the men and offered us a tour of the prison facilities.

We were on our way out of the gate when Melody finally turned to me and asked, "I'm not quite sure what message you were trying to deliver with that; but it was interesting, especially how proud the inmates were as they discussed their personal reformations."

"Melody, we have spent days together over the last month. You are very astute, and I appreciate your reporting skills. You have just spent an hour in an environment where everybody is equal. You can't get much more equality than the same living conditions, same clothes, same food, same entertainment, same exercise, same opportunity for study, same minor privileges. But all three of those men and every other inmate would trade that equality for liberty in a minute. All those stories they discussed, how they were working on reforming themselves, all were targeted at gaining their freedom. They worked hard to tell you how hard they were working to be better citizens, to earn their liberty, something most of us take for granted.

"In the Americas there are three countries where socialist governments have imposed equality. Cuba, Venezuela, and more recently Nicaragua. All went from nations with a solid middle class, an elite upper class, and poor people to equality. But the economic policies of each have yielded equal misery. Venezuela had the highest per-capita income in Latin America. It sits on the largest oil and natural gas reserve in the Americas, but the people now cook over wood fires because the government, in the name of equality, collapsed the economy and drove out the wealthy and the educated, including engineers. Everyone is far more equal than in the past, and miserable."

"You don't see Americans, even socialist Americans, illegally crossing their borders for a better life. But tens of thousands of people from those nations are trying to flee here. They are in a prison, an economic and political prison at home and just like the inmates at Pauch River, they want out.

9

CAN I BUY YOU A BEER?

Two weeks later, after Melody published her last two articles, she called me, late in the afternoon. "Can we meet?" she asked. "Both my publisher and editor are a little unhappy with the tone of my last two articles. My editor buttonholed me last night and asked one question that I couldn't answer."

"Oh?" I replied.

Melody laughed. "If the country, the economy, and the society are all such positives, why are so many people unhappy?"

"Only if we can meet for a beer, I replied, I've had a hell of a day with edits on that political book I'm writing. It's a lot tougher than writing pure historical fiction. Oh, and my old guy upbringing will require me to at least offer to buy."

An hour later we were at the same corner table in the pub where we first met. There were two empty glasses on the table and two full ones.

"Well, enough small talk," I offered, "let's get on to the question your editor asked."

"Great," replied Melody as she munched on the slice of orange from her second Blue Moon beer.

"Three words. Envy. Empathy. Sympathy."

Her face turned to that expression she had when she didn't have clue what I was talking about.

"Envy means a feeling of discontented or resentful longing aroused by someone else's possession's, qualities, or luck. For people who don't really believe that they can reach for the stars, really become successful themselves, seeing others with more or with better opportunities makes them very resentful; they feel deprived. They are envious of others' success and disgruntled by their own lives. If enough of them get together and somehow arrive at the idea that the others didn't earn their success, then together they create a narrative that it is unfair. Like in so many things we have discussed, the media needs problems or conflicts. So, they amplify those feelings to their subscribers and spread feelings driven by envy across the land.

"Now the other two terms, Empathy and Sympathy. Empathy is the ability to understand and share the feelings of another. Sympathy seems the same, but it is not. Sympathy is your personal feelings of sorrow for someone else's misfortune. People feel sympathy, they have empathy.

Those of us who look at other people who have less or whose life could be better and deal with it using empathy, will almost always stop to think about how we might help solve the problem. If we approach it with the mindset of a real American, we realize that what we can do is try to help the less fortunate by exposing opportunity for them to take care of themselves, to grow their awareness and skills; to thrive on their own.

Those who look at the same people with sympathy instead, feel pity for those less fortunate. It makes them upset; they feel bad, guilty. Their focus becomes finding some instant way of resolving the sorrow in their own mind. Giving less fortunate people something that makes their life better right now helps diffuse that guilt. Blaming someone else or some group reduces their personal guilt. Or they demand that society or government do something to alleviate the problem, usually by demanding some form of handout. Their objective is to make the feeling of sorrow go away even if it doesn't lead to a long-term solution. Those receiving a minor handout are better off than before but develop a pattern that robs them of the realization that they can be truly successful. I'm not speaking of all, but the number of less fortunate who buy into believing they are victims is a disaster.

As my friend Dave explains, real Americans always want to improve their lives. They will do it by taking responsible actions and working hard, respecting others. Those driven only by envy, who do not respect their fellow citizens, might just stick a gun in your face and take what you have earned. Their life improvement is temporary. They do not respect their fellow citizens. Those who deal with the less fortunate only with sympathy do something worse. If you get caught stealing the fruits of someone else's time, you will probably go to prison. Like the men we met at Pauch River, you have a chance of learning from mistakes. But if you allow the system to pay you just enough to survive, and lose the drive to thrive, you may never get ahead. Government agencies and a lot of non-profit groups have job security since they never solve the real problem."

"I'm not sure if or how to write that," said Melody.

"And there is the long-term problem," I replied. "It's why I am writing my book. It's a lot like what John told you. Remember, the fastest way to get your house burned down in some inner cities is to disagree with the local church's push for more government aid. Sympathy instead of empathy and government's need to have problems last forever have kept us from long-term solutions for decades. But those of us who write can help—if we have courage."

I left Melody not quite sure of what she was going to do. I was reminded of the late political philosopher Charles Krauthammer's comment. "Conservatives think liberals are stupid and liberals think conservatives are evil." Neither of course is accurate, but without a little gray hair you tend to worry too much about what others might think of you, instead of just doing what you believe is right.

I hoped that Melody, with sandy brown hair that wouldn't turn grey for years would never lose her passion for others. I also hoped that she might help find permanent solutions. It occurred to me that over the past several weeks neither of us tried to label the other or criticize. That was real progress. Now, if I can just work that kind of solution into my new book.

ORIGINS

AWAKE is drawn from a non-fiction book that I wrote earlier, STILL COMMON SENSE. That book includes survey data from both progressive and conservative citizens and a great deal of research. As an author of thriller fiction, most based on some snippet of history that doesn't add up, my research into the nation's history, culture, economy and legal system is ongoing. STILL COMMON SENSE demanded a deeper dive into how America has lost sight of what works in the country and the continual progress the nation is making on difficult problems. AWAKE is a fictional tale drawn from what I learned in writing STILL COMMON SENSE and the feedback offered by the readers of that book. Clearly, the story content of AWAKE, although fiction, is one that every American can find for themselves, if we are willing to go outside the echo-chamber of modern media and social media; if we are willing to talk to one another rather than listen only to those who feel as we feel.

America is not perfect, but a better one than my parents left me and not as good as my children will leave my grandchildren. That country will be very different than most of us would consider perfect today. You own you in an imperfect but exceptional United States of America.

ABOUT THE AUTHOR

RODGER CARLYLE *is a storyteller who draws on an enormous personal library of experiences. An adventurer, political strategist, and ghostwriter whose love of flying began in the Navy, his experiences stretch from New York to Los Angeles, from Amsterdam to Khabarovsk in the Russian Far East, and from Canada into Latin America.*

Through his passion for research, he treasures finding those events that are ignored or covered up by the powerful when some strategy or plan goes completely to hell. From there, he creates a fictional adventure narrative that tells a more complete story.

Rodger is comfortable in black tie urban settings, but he is never happier than in the wilderness. He has faced down muggers in San Francisco, intimidation by the Russian Mafia, and charging grizzly bears. Most of his stories take his readers to places they will never visit. He likes to think that he is there with them.

Visit Rodger Carlyle's website at www.rodgercarlyle.com

www.ingramcontent.com/pod-product-compliance
Lightning Source LLC
Chambersburg PA
CBHW051234210726
48290CB00003B/959